SECRET INVASION

SECRET INVASION

PAUL DELLINGER

FuturesPast Publishing

FuturesPast Publishing
ISBN 13: 978-0990753018

First Edition

Printed in the United States of America

Dedicated to
Grace and Emma Koppelman
granddaughters galore
because they asked

AUTHOR'S NOTE

This story originated as part of the Pulp & Paper 48-Hour Writing Contest held in Roanoke, Virginia in 2013. The challenge was to complete a story of at least 30,000 words within that time period - which amounted to more than 600 words per hour assuming the writer didn't sleep. The contest required the inclusion of certain settings and institutions in the city of Roanoke, and the use of certain phrases and objects in ways significant to the story. These were given to each of the 22 participants at the start of the 48 hours, to make sure no one wrote his or her story in advance of the challenge period. In the middle of the 48 hours, the computer I was using died - literally died. Luckily, I had saved most of the work that far to a flashdrive, and was able to finish on another computer within the time limit. It was an intense and exciting way to produce a story. I hope you enjoy it.

Paul Dellinger
SW Virginia

1–

"But their greatest mystery the heavens have kept a secret. What sort of life, if any, inhabits these other planets? Human life, like ours? Or life extremely lower in the scale? Or dangerously higher?" - *Opening narration,* Invaders from Mars *(1953)*

It was the largest free-standing illuminated man-made star in the world, looking down from more than 1,000 feet on the city of Roanoke, the biggest city in western Virginia. The light from its 2,000 feet of neon tubing put to shame and almost drowned out many of the real stars that twinkled above Mill Mountain. But such perspectives are deceiving. The same human point of view which once made it obvious that the world was flat also made it seem that the artificial star dwarfed those overhead. Not so. Many of those faint sparks in the night sky could have engulfed the city, the planet, the solar system, which all goes to show that that which is obvious is also often wrong.

But the Mill Mountain Star made a convenient point of reference, once something from out there dropped close enough for its shape to be seen.

Several things dropped onto Mill Mountain that night in 1950, one year after the artificial star's construction. Nobody saw them. At least, nobody human.

Below, in the city, movies such as *Cyrano de Bergerac, Harvey, Sunset Boulevard* and even *Destination: Moon* were playing in theaters like the Jefferson, Grandin and Lee. Audiences still not quite used to home television flocked to see them, completely unaware of the even more fantastic story which was beginning at that moment on the mountain to the south.

The unseen objects drifted slowly to earth. If anyone from the city had seen them, that person might have described them as resembling giant eggs – smooth, oval, and lying completely still.

And then, a fissure appeared in the glassy surface of one of them. It widened into an opening. And the first of its occupants began to emerge…

2—

"They're here already! You're next!"
- Kevin McCarthy as Doctor Miles Bennell in Invasion of
the Body Snatchers *(1956)*

    I had taken a cab from Roanoke Regional Airport, which I still thought of as Woodrum Field, to the Hotel Roanoke and Conference Center. I still thought of it simply as the Hotel Roanoke. I hadn't been back to the city since its multi-million restoration in the 1990s, and I was impressed. The multi-story building towered over the circular driveway and its alcove entrance. As I was reaching for my suitcase, the Yellow Cab in which I was riding jerked to a stop.

The driver turned around to me. "What kind of convention did you say this was?" he asked.

I looked up and saw, standing in conversation on the sidewalk outside the entrance, a pointy-eared Vulcan, a guy in a silver coverall with a purple face and antenna atop his head, and a pretty green-haired girl in a mini-skirt and what looked like a brass brassiere. And then I understood the question.

"It's a science fiction convention," I told him again. "You know – Spider-Man, *Avatar*, John Carter." He continued looking at me blankly. "Buck Rogers? Flash Gordon? *Star Trek*?" That was when the light dawned.

"Oh. Okay. And *Star Wars*, I guess," he said. "My kid made me sit through it with him six times when he was little. Come to think of it, these people do look like refugees from the bar scene."

I got out with my bag, paid the driver, and walked in to the lobby and registration desk. "Simon Carr," I said, identifying myself. "I have a reservation."

The young man behind the desk quickly came up with my room number and key card. "I hope you enjoy your stay with us, Mr. Carr," he said. "It may be a little hectic for the next few days. The hotel is hosting a science fiction convention."

"So I see," I said, looking at the row of tables against a wall on one side of the lobby, where mostly young folks in all manner of clothing were lined up. "In fact, I'm attending it, myself."

The clerk almost managed to hide his surprise. I guess I didn't look much like most of the attendees. I was wearing a sports coat and tie, my hair was just starting to go gray at the temples, and I didn't have pointy ears. "Oh, are you one of the guest authors?" he asked.

"Nope. Just another Trekkie," I said, and left him to puzzle it out to his satisfaction. My room was on the third floor and, rather than join the line at the nearest elevator, I found a nearby door to the stairway and walked up.

The room was great, the large bed covered with all kinds of pillows, a couple comfortable-looking chairs, a desk, and, most important for the reason I was here, free room internet access. It didn't take me long to unpack, and to set up my laptop computer so I'd be ready to send stuff to the newspaper. The *Roanoke Times* building was actually not that far away, but there was no sense in walking to a computer station there when I could do everything from here. Besides, it took a magnetic-strip badge to get into the paper's building these days, and I no longer qualified for one.

Well, I reflected, all the household chores were taken care of. Time to register for Star-Con, the most prestigious SF convention ever to hit the Star City of the South. And it had plenty of competition…RoVaCon, SheVaCon, MystiCon, Point North, and probably others I hadn't heard of. Roanoke was the only place I knew which hosted two SF conventions in the same month. And a number of them had been hosted in this very same hotel, both before and after its restoration.

"Simon Carr." I gave my name again, this time to the smiling but harried young lady at the table for attendees registered in advance. She dug through the various stacks of paper in front of her, and came up with a convention booklet, a handful of flyers advertising everything from comic book stores to other conventions, and a badge with my name which I was supposed to wear to get into any of the con activities this evening and over the next two days.

"I hope you enjoy it, Mr. Carr," she said. "Some of the author and artist guests are already here, too. Our media guests, Luke Larabee and Dana DuQueen, won't be available until this evening, but they'll be at the opening ceremonies."

I recognized the names as the stars of the latest sci-fi television series, on some independent channel I couldn't immediately recall. I couldn't even think of the name of their show, which was pitiful for someone who had grown up reading this stuff and attending every SF movie that came out. Dana DuQueen, judging by her image on the cardboard placard standing behind the registration tables, was a stunning-looking blonde with a couple other Dolly Parton attributes besides her tousled hair. I remembered Luke Larabee mainly from some westerns I'd seen on TV as well as the big screen, but I didn't think they were making many of those, anymore. Too bad – he had a nice Sam Elliott-style delivery which suited them perfectly.

I found a seat on one end of a couch in the lobby, and opened the convention booklet to the pages showing the schedule of events. A dealers' room was in the process of being set up down a hallway branching off from the lobby, but it wasn't open yet. No events were scheduled until 6 p.m., so I would have time for a meal before things got underway.

The line at the elevator was shorter this time, so I rode up to the third floor with two other passengers, both men, neither of them appearing to be fellow conventioneers. As we rode up, a high-pitched screech like fingernails across a chalkboard permeated the car, and then was gone. We all looked at each other, and smiled uneasily.

The door slid open, and the three of us came face to face with a wild-eyed young man whose skin had a pale-blue tinge all over, and who was making inarticulate sounds as he grabbed at us with claw-like fingers. His stringy blond hair stuck out in all directions, and his eyes seemed to be bugging out of his head. He looked like a strung-out refugee from *West Side Story*, or one of Leo Gorcey's "East Side Kids."

Nobody seemed to know how to respond to this apparition. "What is it? What's wrong?" I managed to say.

He kept trying to speak, but nothing intelligible came out. A few of the words might have been "imposter" or "alien," and something that sounded like "scrambled brain cells," but I could never have been sure.

Then he let out a short burst of a scream, and dropped at our feet.

3—

Rex Reason as Doctor Cal Meacham: "Sun lamp?"
Faith Domergue as Doctor Ruth Adams: "That's what it
looks like. Only instead of a suntan, you get your brain
cells rearranged." - This Island, Earth *(1953)*

The call had come from Trem Bagley, the only editor I remembered who was still working at the Roanoke newspaper.

"Hello, Simon. How would you like to fly down to Roanoke and do a special assignment for us for three days and some good pay?"

I held the receiver away from my ear, looked at it, then put it back. "Who is this?" I demanded.

"It's me, Bagley. Metro editor. Used to be city editor. Come on, Simon, it hasn't been that long."

Actually, it had been almost a decade, and I was surprised that Bagley was still there. Bagley had been an old-school editor, just the facts, ma'am, who-what-where-when-why-how and none of those featurized soft news lead-ins to a story. Somehow, he must have survived the transition to digital media, and the more story-telling approach to news designed to draw in readers with lots of other news sources competing for their attention.

"I'm doing all right up here in Yankee-land, Bagley. Highland Falls is close enough to New York for me to get to what magazine offices are still around, and I've got West Point right around the corner from me if I need a parade. Besides, have you forgotten? I was fired down there a long time ago."

And it had been my own damned fault, I knew. Cheyanne Caday had certainly been worth it, but the editors rightly frowned upon the kind of fraternization she and I had been doing, when I was a reporter and she was one of the public relations people for a member of the Virginia House of Delegates. I was sure in my own mind that I had always been entirely objective in everything I had written about her delegate. I didn't think any of our readers would even be able to tell whether I had voted for him or not. But when word of our liaisons leaked out, as we should both have known it would, eventually, the appearance of a possible conflict of interest was enough to get me my walking papers.

"We're not offering to re-hire you, Simon," Bagley said. "But this is something that's perfect for you, and not for any of us. You were always big into that sci-fi crap, weren't you?"

I cringed at his reference to "sci-fi," a term which a guy named Forrest Ackerman had coined to correspond to "hi-fi," but which had come to mean schlock science fiction, usually in B-movies, to a number of militant SF fans.

But he was right. When I was growing up, I spent my

quarters at my hometown's newsstand for practically every SF paperback that came out onto the store's spinner-rack. Back then, you could literally buy every one of them, maybe one or two a month, nothing like the rows of science fiction and fantasy you found in bookstores these days. I probably saw every movie from 1950 on, too, at least until my time in college, and then the Army, and then in newspapering. Now, I didn't have time to see many of them. Just about every other special-effects picture coming out these days seemed to have some sort of SF or fantasy angle, from James Bond to Harry Potter. These days, I probably read more mystery novels than SF ones.

Back when I'd started reading the stuff, it had – for want of a better term – a sense of wonder about it, a description I'd heard so many old-time readers use. Anything was possible. There just might be life on Mars, or prehistoric swamplands on Venus. You could park an Oz-like setting on any planet you could name, or make up a name for, and nobody could say absolutely that it could not be. We could defy the light barrier and travel to other stars through hyperspace. We could move through time itself. Now, we knew so much more, and the stories had to stick to at least some semblance of the new astronomy or physics, and the ones I'd tried lately read more like technical papers than unfettered adventure extravaganzas I remembered.

"Simon? You there?"

"Yeah, I'm here. How did you track me down, anyway?"

"Don't be modest. You've done all right as a freelancer. That's why I thought you might be open to a freelance gig down here at your old stomping grounds."

"I can't imagine anything down there that your own staff couldn't cover as well as I could."

"How about a big-name science fiction convention?" he asked.

"What's so big about that? There have been cons all over the country, at least since the late '30s. I don't guess a week goes by that there's not one somewhere in the country. And Roanoke's been having them since 1976."

I knew the year, because I had attended that one, RoVaCon I, organized by members of the Nelson Bond Society, named for an author who lived in Roanoke and who had written across every kind of pulp and slick magazine genre, including SF. One of the guest authors – call him John Jones – had visited the local Waldenbooks store and threw a tantrum because it had none of his paperbacks in the SF section.

"How come you don't have any of my books, by John Jones?" he demanded of the girl at the sales desk.

"Oh, we must have just run out of them," she said demurely. "We will order a bunch of them right away. We always try to stock books by John Jones."

Mollified, the author stalked away. I stayed behind long enough to see the girl turn to another store employee, and say in a low voice, "Who the hell is John Jones?"

I had been a young reporter at the Roanoke Times, back when there was also an afternoon paper, the Roanoke World-News, when that convention was held. I covered it for several years, and got to interview a number of writers and artists, including Nelson Bond himself. But each time it was just another story among hundreds all of us at the paper would write each year, and I had all but forgotten about it.

"This is a new convention," Bagley said. "Star-Con, they're calling it. I guess the name derives from the Mill Mountain Star, I don't know. Anyway, they have somehow finagled some big-time guests, like Maurice Allgood, and Professor Chiswell, both of whom are supposed to make some big-news announcements at this convention."

I'd heard of them both. Professor M. F. Chiswell was managing to appear on all the cable news shows these days because of a book he'd written about UFOs. I hadn't read it, so I wasn't sure what all the fuss was about, because it seemed like there were almost as many UFO books out there as there were SF books. Doctor Allgood was a different story. He was a key researcher in the search for extraterrestrial life, and had the charisma of an Issac Asimov or a Carl Sagan, so I could see why Bagley would want him covered.

"So what's the problem? It's right there in your back yard," I said.

"The problem is that they're not allowing any reporter access. They're not letting anybody in except convention members. So I thought, if you'd attend the convention…"

"That doesn't make any sense. Why would either of them want to make high-profile announcements and not get coverage?"

"Oh, they'll have coverage. All the cable news people will be there. Even our own Channel 7 and Channel 10 will be allowed. But whoever's running the convention seems to have a grudge against newspapers."

"That would be me," I said. "How did you know I was running the con?"

A few seconds of silence followed. I think Bagley almost believed me. Then he laughed. "Look, Simon, I doubt if anybody here at the paper now even remembers your little peccadillo. And even if they did, the guy you were writing about hasn't been in office for years. And this Star-Con is about as far removed from local politics as anything could get. You know we don't often use freelancers, so you should feel honored. All expenses paid, plus what we'd pay you as a special reporter. Think about it."

As it happened, I was between assignments right now, and I could use a little extra income. And it might even be fun to see the old home place again. Allgood by himself might be worth the trip, as omnipresent as he was lately in the media. Chiswell might be a crackpot, or there might be more to him than I knew. It actually sounded interesting, and I wouldn't be investing anything but my time.

"What exactly would you want me to do? Just cover whatever they announce?"

"Well, a little more than that," Bagley said. "Since our arts and entertainment reporter can't get in, maybe you could send us some stuff about some of the celebrities besides these two that we could put out on-line. I think they have a couple of movie stars attending, too."

"On-line?"

"Oh yeah, we're big-time into the digital age. Have been for several years. Constantly putting updates out on our internet blogs and such. Twenty-four hour news cycle, and all that. We can use as much stuff as you can give us."

"Won't the newspaper-haters in charge figure out that you've slipped a mole into their setup when the stuff starts appearing?" I asked.

"Well, we won't give you a byline, that's all. I mean, this is more up-front cash than we've ever put up for a freelance gig, so far as I can remember. If you're getting that much money, you don't need glory, too, do you?"

"I think you're just pissed about them trying to exclude you," I said. I actually did remember Bagley pretty well, and I knew how he would react to that.

"Maybe I am. So, listen up. Here are the dates, the place, and all that." He filled me in, and I jotted it all down on a pad of paper on my desk. "Are you in?"

"Okay, I guess so. You want mainly whatever Allgood and Chiswell are releasing, but little min-pieces on various and sundry other guests. I can do that. But I can't believe it's worth what you'll be paying me. Hell, whenever I covered any of those cons before, I had to persuade you to even let them go in the paper. You thought it was a dumb use of space."

"Well, sci-fi seems to be a bigger deal these days. I don't pretend to understand it, but I don't understand much about newspaper work anymore. We kicked around whether to ignore this thing or actually try to get something out of it, I thought of you, and the other editors went along. Anything else you need to know?"

"Yeah. Your email address, for one, if that's where I'm going to be sending stuff. And if there's any kind of a schedule you want to be getting these bits and pieces. And your phone number, in case I can think of anything else to ask about."

And so, within a few days, I was on an airplane to Roanoke with several reporter's notebooks, a laptop, and a small cassette tape recorder for backup. I hadn't ever used a cassette recorder back when I was with the paper. I relied on my notes, and the bastardized shorthand I'd invented for myself. All that a tape recording meant was that I would have to listen to the same thing twice and, at the rate we used to churn out news stories, I seldom had time for that. But, since I'd been freelancing and detail was more important than getting something first, fast and factually, I'd gone through several recorders over the years. The one I had now was small enough to fit into my shirt pocket, but sensitive enough to pick up words without air-conditioning or other background noises interfering too much with them. It had come in handy on several occasions, and I could see where it would do so again on this assignment, where people might be talking about things in which I had no background. Last of the generalists, that was me.

But, before I could even think about filing anything, I was face to face with someone who looked like he'd either been zapped by a freeze-ray, was suffering from some unknown sort of plague, or had just made himself up to look like a sci-fi horror to see how many of the elevator people he could frighten. If that last thing was what he was after, he had certainly managed to frighten me.

4—

"An intellectual carrot. The mind boggles."
- Douglas Spencer as Ned "Scotty" Scott, The Thing (from Another World), *1951*

The boy lay face down, arms splayed out, body shaking as though made of some sort of gelatin. I dashed for my room, inserted the key, made a quick call to the desk downstairs, and grabbed the heavy reddish-colored spread off the bottom of my bed. I brought it back to the elevator, where the other two people still stood, and covered the shaking body with it. I could only think that the kid must be in shock, and it was important to keep him warm.

The people at the desk must have been pretty efficient.

They not only had some hotel personnel up there within minutes, but they located a doctor who examined the boy briefly and ordered him hospitalized.

"Take him to Roanoke Community," the doctor, who was probably younger than I was, told the emergency services people who carefully moved the boy onto a stretcher. "I'll meet you there."

"Hey, this guy's cold!" one of the emergency crew said. "He feels like an ice cube."

"Keep him warm," the doctor said. Turning to me, he added, "That blanket was a good idea. It may have helped."

"What's the matter with him?" I asked.

"I've never seen anything like it," he said.

One of the emergency technicians took down my name and room number, as well as those of the other two guys from the elevator, who were still standing there open-mouthed. "I don't know who, but I'm sure somebody's going to want to talk to each of you," he said.

I went to my room, hoping that whatever the guy had wasn't contagious. My hands felt cold where I'd touched him. I wasn't sure how much of that was my imagination, because of what the emergency guy had said. I stripped and went to the room's shower, with the hot water turned up as high as I could stand it.

Did this rate a call to Bagley? I couldn't really write a story about it, beyond the fact that an unidentified young man had staggered into a hallway of the hotel looking as though he was half-frozen and mouthing strange nonsensical words. But maybe Bagley could have a reporter at the hospital who could find out more.

So I called the number he had given me. I got his recording. I booted up my laptop, pecked out everything I knew, and sent it off to his email address.

Then I dressed, informally – black jeans, tennis shoes, light-blue shirt – and made my way back to the elevator. From the ground-floor lobby, I strolled around a few corners until I came to The Regency Room, which looked inviting with its white-linen covering the tables, curtained windows, and decorative wall lighting. I had planned to eat large on the paper's expense account, but I found I wasn't that hungry, anymore. I settled for Caesar salad and crab soup.

I had just finished, and was about to go see how far things had progressed in setting up the dealers' room, when I found myself facing a heavy-set balding man wearing a dark-blue suit, striped tie and an unhappy frown. "Are you Simon Carr?" he demanded.

"Yeah, that's right."

"Investigator Delaney, Roanoke city police. Like to talk with you a few minutes, Mr. Carr. Want to go up to your room? I was just looking for you there."

"I just came from there. To here," I said.

"Well, we can go over to Campbell Avenue and talk at the department, but I'd think your room would be more convenient for you."

I thought so, too. Back to the elevator we went, and I found myself mentally preparing for something scary when its door slid open on my floor. But there was nothing and nobody there this time. I unlocked my room, and we sat down facing each other in its two large chairs.

"Okay, Mr. Carr. Just tell me in your own words what happened."

I told him. He took some notes, but mainly he listened. It didn't take me long to give what little information I had, and he leaned back in his chair, pondering it for several minutes before he spoke.

"Do you know the boy? Had you ever seen him before?"

"No. I don't even know his name."

"He had a tag pinned on his shirt with the name 'Jimmy Cox,'" Delaney said. "That mean anything to you?"

"The name doesn't. The tag probably means he was attending this science fiction convention that starts here tonight."

"This whole darn thing seems like science fiction," Delaney said. "They still haven't figured out what's the matter with him. It's like he spent the day in a freezer somewhere."

"Is he going to make it?"

"His temperature is slowly getting back to normal. They hope he'll be stabilized soon. But he hasn't regained consciousness, so we still don't know what happened to him."

"I wish I could help you, Mr. Delaney. But I've told you everything I know."

Delaney almost smiled. "Well, at least it's more than your companions in the elevator could tell us. Oh, and I'll get that bedding that you used to keep him warm back to you as soon as I can. Wouldn't want you to have to pay for it," he said.

"I appreciate that."

Delaney asked a few general questions about me, where I was from, what I was doing here. I told him part of the truth – that I was from here, that I'd enjoyed science fiction conventions in the past, that I had some time off and thought I'd see what this one was like.

"You a sci-fi writer or something?" he asked.

I laughed. "I'm a writer, but just articles, not fiction. I used to be on the Roanoke newspaper, years ago."

"Okay." He stood up and put his tablet inside his coat. "Well, enjoy yourself. I might want to talk to you again before you leave." On that less-than-reassuring note, he took his leave.

After he was gone, I looked through the program book and figured I'd better skip the dealers' room for now if I wanted to get to the opening ceremonies. They were due to start in the Washington Lecture Hall, which was on the lobby floor according to the book's map of the hotel. I pocketed my little cassette recorder, stuck a ballpoint pen and small tablet in my shirt pocket, pinned on my Star-Con badge, and set out.

The master of ceremonies was a vest full of buttons with various sayings on them over a red-and-white Roanoke Rebels jersey, and a Robin Hood cap with what looked like a turkey feather sticking out of it. If he had a clothing theme, it was beyond me. He gave a short welcoming speech, and then started calling out names.

The fact that I recognized only a few of the writers' names and none of the artists' brought home to me how long I had been out of the SF loop. I may have accepted Bagley's offer under false pretenses, if genre expertise was what he expected. But I reasoned that it had been more important to him to get someone inside, and the fact that I had attended a number of previous cons in Roanoke gave me credentials of sorts to get there.

"And now," the M.C. called out, "the stars of TV's latest science fiction series, *The Planet Pawns*! Luke Larabee, who plays The Knight, and Dana DuQueen, who, naturally, plays The Queen. Let's give them a big hand!"

The audience responded enthusiastically, and the two stars with the alliterative names came running onto the stage at the front of the hall. Luke Larabee looked a bit older to me than I remembered when I'd last seen him perform, and Dana DuQueen looked shorter than I would have guessed – but, I had to admit, everything was in fine proportion. She wore a red tunic on top and a white mini-skirt, reminding me somewhat of a high school cheerleader. Luke was dressed more conservatively, in jeans trousers and a jeans jacket.

They each gave a little glad-to-be-here speech and a plug for *Planet Pawns* (even the title of their show was alliterative). I didn't bother to switch on the recorder or take any notes. I was mainly waiting to hear what Allgood or Chiswell might have to say, when the M.C. got around to introducing them.

I looked around the chamber and realized that fully a quarter of the attendees wore costumes of some sort – not just science fictional, but there was a little girl dressed like Alice in Wonderland, at least three Dracula types, a Conan-style barbarian or two, a guy in a blue suit and glasses with his shirt pulled open to reveal a Superman "S" underneath, a Catwoman, a Wicked Witch out of Oz, a Lone Ranger based on the Disney mode, an older gentleman wearing a T-shirt that said "Back in my day, we had nine planets," a pirate, and even a giant orange carrot which stood in the aisle on two very attractive and shapely legs.

For a minute, I felt sure the carrot was looking back at me. I could barely make out two little eyelets so its wearer could see where she – with those legs, it had to be a she – was going.

The next thing I knew, the carrot was walking toward me down the row of seats where I had put myself. It came all the way over to the vacant seat next to me, sat down, crossed its legs and leaned toward me. A tiny slot popped open just below the eye-holes, about where the wearer's mouth should be.

"Hello, Simon," a familiar voice said. "Long time, no see."

5—

Margaret Field, as Enid: "You know, I think that creature was friendly. I wonder what would have happened if – if Doctor Mears hadn't frightened him."

Robert Clarke, as John: "Who knows? Perhaps the greatest curse ever to befall the world, or perhaps the greatest blessing." - The Man from Planet X *(1951)*

I would have known the voice of Cheyanne Caday whether I heard it on Mars, Mercury or Mongo. But I never expected to recognize it here.

"Annie?" I whispered back. "What in the world are you doing here?"

"I might ask you the same question," she said. "But I guess we're both here for the fun of it."

It did make a kind of sense. Our common interest in science fiction was what got Cheyanne and me interested in one another, in the first place. I remembered her telling me how she was still angry at her grade school librarian for not letting her check out the SF books she had wanted because, the librarian informed her, "those are *boys'* books."

"Hey," she said. "I've been wondering for years. Why didn't you ever write? Or call? I didn't even know where you were until I ran across a magazine article you'd written."

"They'd already fired me," I said. "But they agreed not to make anything of it if I went quietly. If I showed up on your doorstep again, I was afraid you'd run into the same situation and you might get fired, too."

I heard her familiar little laugh echoing inside her carrot costume. "I'd probably have gotten promoted," she said. "If they really believed I was sleeping with the press to get better coverage."

I'd never thought of that. Mentally, I kicked myself for being so needlessly noble and letting Cheyanne drift out of my life.

"What are you doing now?" I asked.

Again came the laugh. "What does it look like? Can't you guess what character I'm symbolically representing? James Arness as the carrot creature?"

"I don't mean right now. I mean, are you still doing public relations work? Your delegate hasn't been in Richmond for a long time."

"Oh, I've moved on several times since then. I guess my top job was as an aide to our last congressman, and did he keep me busy! But I'm glad I'm not in Washington now, with the gridlock they've got going on these days. We used to get good stuff done, but not anymore."

"No more public relations?" I asked.

"Oh, yes. I've been plenty busy this past year or so, trying to line up appearances for Maurice Allgood. I guess you've heard of him."

I guessed I had. "You're with Doctor Allgood now?"

"You sound surprised."

"No wonder he's getting such good coverage everywhere. You always were good at your job."

"Thanks. I guess. All this time, I thought you must be angry at me for getting you fired."

"It was my own fault. If I'd gone to an editor and said I had a relationship with you, and so couldn't cover your legislator anymore…"

"But state politics was your beat back then. How could you not cover someone like that? I mean, a lot of things were happening in the General Assembly at the time."

"I should have figured some way. And I should have known the rumor mill would out us, sooner or later."

"I wish it could have been later."

I wasn't sure what to say to that, so I changed the subject. "I hadn't even thought of Doctor Allgood having a P.R. staff."

"Somebody's got to get his books and pronouncements and discoveries out there. Wait until you hear what he has to say during his guest of honor speech tomorrow night."

"What's it about?"

"Can't tell you," she said. "Conflict of interest." And we both laughed. "Oh, look, here he comes now."

"…one of our best-known researchers in the realm of the extraterrestrial," the M.C. was saying. "Doctor Allgood has already been a leader in studies indicating that there really could have once been life on Mars, and maybe still is. And he has chosen Star-Con as the place where he will be making another earth-shaking, or should I say planet-shaking, announcement, and we're all wondering what that's going to be. Let's have a round of applause for Doctor Allgood."

Cheyanne couldn't very well applaud, with her arms encased in her carrot costume. I gave a few claps after I'd surreptitiously switched on my cassette recorder. I hoped Cheyanne hadn't noticed. Surely that carrot shell would have limited her peripheral vision.

Or maybe not. "What are you doing?" she whispered.

"I'm interested in what he's going to say," I said.

"Thank you, all, for that warm welcome," Allgood said, taking center stage. He was not tall but compact, with hair so black that I suspected its color had some artificial help. He had piercing blue eyes, and a smile so bright that I suspected artifice there, too. But he was an impressive figure, and I could see why television cameras loved him.

"Science fiction fans have always been better than think tanks or futurists at predictions," he said. "Your statisticians can choose a trend and try to project how it will change and what it will become over time. But they cannot factor in some off-the-wall event like, say, a spaceship landing in Washington. And it is those unexpected developments that truly shape the futures in which all of us will live. I hope that many of you will be able to attend my little talk tomorrow evening, when I will give you one of those off-the-wall happenings which none of the experts have anticipated. And what better place to announce something like that than a place like Star-Con?" He sat down to even more thunderous applause.

Next up was Professor M. F. Chiswell. I didn't think I'd ever heard exactly what he was a professor of, but the M.C. was still giving him an enthusiastic introduction, going on about his revelations concerning flying saucers, the "actual" photographs of aerial phenomena that he had gathered from various sources and published in his most recent book, and the fact that he, too, had scheduled a promised revelation of some kind in his guest of honor speech tomorrow night, immediately following that of astronomer and researcher Allgood. The M.C. added that StarCon was the first gathering anywhere in the country boasting head-to-head talks, each with a surprise, by both Allgood and Chiswell.

And then, the professor strode out to center stage. He actually looked, to me, like the caricature of a stereotypical professor, probably the kind who was absent-minded as well. He was tall, gawky, on the skinny side, with frizzy Einsteinian hair and heavy-lidded eyes that made you think he was on the verge of sleep. He wore a shapeless gray sweater, but I couldn't help picturing him more in a white laboratory coat.

"Yes, Doctor Allgood and I both have things to tell you," he began. "I have no idea what Doctor Allgood's news may be, but my own will literally shake the world."

My carrot's mouth-hole popped open again. "Jealousy, jealousy," Cheyanne said. "More UFO stuff, I'll bet. You'd think people would stop taking him seriously, after a while, with all those claims and no evidence ever to back them up."

I tended to agree. I'd seen glimpses enough of Chiswell making extravagant claims of various kinds on TV shows, but I never remembered him backing them up. He would just move on to some new claim, and viewers apparently would just forget about the last one.

"We have all seen motion pictures depicting aliens from other worlds as evil, or fearsome, but has it ever occurred to you that inhabitants of other worlds could be more afraid of us than we are of them? And what might they do in such a situation? This is part of what I will be speaking about tomorrow night, but

I will provide you with a little preview of that revelation right now…"

A high-pitched screech, like feedback from a microphone on steroids, rocked the room. My hands shot to my ears, and I saw others around me having the same reaction. It occurred to me that Cheyanne, in that carrot casing, probably couldn't raise her hands. My own head was pounding, and I could only imagine what she must be going through.

The sound stopped, and a blue light which seemed to emanate somewhere overhead shot onto the stage like a half-seen searchlight beam. And then it, too was gone. But Professor Chiswell stood where it had shown, limbs suddenly askew, shaking as though with palsy. He seemed to be trying to speak, to say something more, but only grunts and inarticulate sounds came out.

And then his legs gave way and he dropped slowly to the floor. It seemed to me, in the glimpse I had of his face before he landed on the stage, that it had turned a pale blue.

6—

Sam Jaffe as Professor Barnhardt: "Have you tested this theory?"
Michael Rennie as Klaatu: "I find it works well enough to get me from one planet to another." - The Day the Earth Stood Still *(1951)*

The room erupted in two directions. Perhaps a third of its occupants bolted for the doors leading to the hotel's hallway. Another third stood shock-still. The others ran toward the prone figure on the stage.

There were cries of "Is there a doctor in the house?" but none appeared. I found myself asking people around me for their coats or other garments to wrap around the professor. I didn't really know why, except that my gut-level reaction to doing that with the kid outside the elevator seemed to have helped him survive whatever had happened to him. And keeping someone warm was standard treatment for shock. If the professor wasn't in shock, I certainly was.

Again, the hotel people responded, along with the same doctor. Again, the victim was sent to Community Hospital. And this time, it wasn't just me and two other people who were instructed to stay on the premises, but the entire room.

I made my way back to where Cheyanne had been sitting, hoping her eardrums had survived that piercing screech. I could still hear ringing from it in my own ears. But when I reached the place where we had been sitting, nobody was there.

I looked all over the room, but nowhere did I see a fugitive carrot with legs.

After a hasty conference with a group which I surmised to be the convention organizers, the M.C. announced that further programming for the evening was cancelled, but that everything set for the next day would be up and running on schedule. He didn't say anything about the time slot reserved for Professor Chiswell's planned talk, but I doubted that the professor would make it.

I looked around for Doctor Allgood, thinking that Cheyanne might be somewhere in his vicinity. But there was no sign of him among the onlookers, either. Seeing Cheyanne here, after all this time, had knocked me off my pins a bit. It only occurred to me now to wonder, if she was here working, what she had been doing in some sort of costume.

With no other obvious options, I retreated to my room and booted up my computer. I composed a story about some unknown force, which manifested itself in an ear-splitting sound and a ray of bluish light, striking down a young con member, Jimmy Cox, and a major convention guest, Professor Chiswell.

I said Roanoke police were investigating the source of the strange manifestation. Considering how few facts I had to work with, I considered it a pretty good account of what had happened and why the convention activities were suspended until the next morning.

I gave it a read-through, changed a few things, typed in Bagley's email address, and hit "send."

Then I closed the computer, unplugged it, put it in a drawer, and waited for a phone call. It wasn't long in coming.

"What is all this shit you're sending me?" Bagley's voice came across the line. "Have you gone completely nuts, Simon?"

"You brought me in to feed you about what happened at the convention," I said. "This is what happened."

"Other-worldly sounds? Blue rays? People being struck down and hospitalized, just as one of them was about to say something about outer space visitors or something? It sounds like you've been infected by some sci-fi virus yourself!" He paused, then went on in a calmer tone: "Simon, you're not still angry about the paper letting you go, are you? You wouldn't deliberately feed me something that would make it a laughing-stock…"

"Bagley, you can believe me or not. That's what happened, damn it." I had a sudden thought. "Hang on, I'll let you hear it for yourself. I recorded it!"

There was an even longer pause. "All right. Go ahead."

I took out my cassette recorder. It was still running. I hit "rewind" and went back to the start of the tape. Then I turned up the volume, held it up to the receiver, and pressed "play."

I finally had to fast forward through Allgood's talk and get to Chiswell, because Bagley was getting impatient. But it was all there, the start of Chiswell's talk, the sound, although muted somewhat on the recording which probably couldn't handle all the decibels it put out, and then the screams and running sounds and comments about how Chiswell looked at the doctor ordering him hospitalized...

I hit the "stop" button. "Satisfied?" I asked.

"I don't see how you could have staged all that," he conceded. "All right, I'll take a chance. Am I going to see any of this on television tonight?"

"No TV cameras here, yet, that I saw. I guess they're saving themselves for the big scheduled talks tomorrow."

"So we'll be hanging out there all by our lonesome on this. I wish we had some kind of official verification."

"Didn't you send anybody to Roanoke Community earlier? Send someone now, and you can at least confirm that the two victims have been admitted, even if they won't give out conditions or what ails them. And you can ask someone at the police department about it. You'll probably get a 'no comment,' but, in a way, that would be verification since it's not an outright denial that any of this happened. Hell, Bagley, do I have to tell you your job? You're the editor I remember never settling for a 'no comment' from anybody."

"Okay, don't get snotty. We're on it. I'll talk to you tomorrow, unless someone from the copy desk has more questions tonight about your story."

"I'm sure this story is going to raise a lot more questions than it answers," I said.

After we hung up, another thought struck me. I called the desk and asked to be connected with another guest, Cheyanne Caday. They put me through, but all I got was the hotel recording saying no one was there just now. At least I'd confirmed that she was staying at this hotel.

Since I was still playing newspaper reporter, I figured I should get out of my room and see what else might be going on downstairs, what kind of reactions people were having, if anyone had any new information on what had gone on. If

Bagley and the copy desk needed to reach me, they had my cell phone.

I could probably have used a good stiff drink. Gone were the days when reporters went across the street after the night shift to the late lamented Ponce de Leon Hotel, and its so-called Pipe Room, where pipes extended from one side of the room to the other, and where alcoholic beverages were served to staffers who had just completed the "daily miracle," getting out another issue of the paper.

I settled for coffee instead, in the hotel's Pine Room Pub which would be open until midnight. The dining room would close at 10, so there was no point in settling in there. And I hoped, too, that I might catch a glimpse of Cheyanne if she was somewhere other than in her room. Maybe she would need to kick back, too.

I didn't find Cheyanne, but I did see her boss, holding forth at the head of a little circular table surrounded by admirers wearing StarCon badges. Although the hum of other conversations drowned out part of what he was saying, I did gather that he wondered if the whole business in the Washington Lecture Hall hadn't been staged by Chiswell himself. That was a possibility which would have appealed to me, actually, if I hadn't seen that kid outside the elevator earlier today.

I walked over to the bar, and got a refill I really didn't need on my coffee, all so I could come back and sit a little closer to where Allgood was addressing his fans. It helped. I could now hear everything he was saying and everything he was asked.

"But suppose it wasn't rigged?" one young naysayer in a Han Solo T-shirt was asking. "If it was real, what could it have been?"

"You mean what if I owe our UFO expert an apology?" Allgood said cheerfully. "I really do hope it was a trick of some kind. I would hate to think he'd actually been laid low by some force or other."

"But if he was?" the kid persisted. "What could do something like that?"

"Well, nothing that I know about," Allgood admitted. "If that phenomenon tonight was something real, either the Pentagon is experimenting with technology that we know nothing about, or there really is someone or something here among us from out there." He let that sink in, as the mouths of most of his listeners formed tiny little o's. "But I wouldn't worry about it," he added reassuringly. "As Carl Sagan said, 'Extraordinary claims require extraordinary evidence.' The simplest explanation is usually the best."

7—

I was down at the Regency Room as soon as it opened
for breakfast the next morning, and chose food from the buffet.
I took my time, hoping Cheyanne would show up. Except for
her legs, I hadn't even seen her last night. For all I knew, she
would no longer be a brunette, and certainly she wouldn't have
the same hair style after all this time. Had she changed? Would

I even recognize her? But she had recognized me without any trouble.

Hell, a good-looking woman like Cheyanne, she was probably married by now. Surely I wasn't operating under the illusion that we could pick up where we'd left off. After all, I was the one who had moved away from her, even if I thought I was doing it for the noblest of reasons. Stupid, I thought. Just stupid.

Gradually, the room filled up. Young people wearing their convention badges, writer and artist guests wearing their more elaborate badges, but no sign of Cheyanne or, for that matter, Doctor Allgood. Maybe they'd decided to eat somewhere away from the hotel for a change of scenery.

After an hour and a half, I gave it up. I walked out to the lobby, where I bought a copy of *The Roanoke Times* and took it to my room. My story had been watered down, but it made the front page. No byline, as I'd expected, just a notation that it was "From staff and special reports." The staff part was well deserved. Somebody had gotten conditions of the two hospital patients, as "guarded but stable." And a city police spokeswoman actually confirmed the strange events of yesterday and last night, adding only that the investigation was continuing to find out what caused them.

The convention booklet showed a few panels scheduled for early in the morning, but nothing I felt worth covering: topics like writing time travel stories or whether comic strips were here to stay. But there was one at 10 a.m. that I wanted to sit in on, where the stars of *Planet Pawns* would be discussing their new show. It didn't particularly interest me, what with all the SF shows on television these days, but I figured it would interest Bagley, since it had the movie star angle.

With all that had happened, I almost wondered if I had imagined the woman in the carrot costume to be Cheyanne. But, no, I had confirmed that she had a room in the hotel. And I didn't imagine our conversation, brief as it had been. Her way of giving off a little burst of laughter when she was amused, that hadn't changed, either. But was I going to get to see her again before this weekend was over and we'd gone our separate ways again?

We'd met on the political beat, but it wasn't politics that got us talking so eagerly to one another. As soon as we realized we'd grown up reading the same books and seeing the same movies, well, everything just grew from there. Besides being extremely pretty, Cheyanne was bright, witty, and knew the most extraordinary bits of information, from what stuntman doubled the star of the *Captain Marvel* movie serial to what woman wrote The *Scarlet Pimpernel* and how the dual identity in that early 20th century play and novel paved the way for Zorro's, Superman's and Batman's foppish alter egos. She knew the names of the four moons that Galileo spotted through his primitive telescope orbiting Jupiter, and she could sing a Broadway tune from every musical play I'd ever heard of. I had the feeling that a lifetime wouldn't be long enough to cover all she had learned. And I had walked away. What had I been thinking?

The first time we kissed was in the back row of a sparsely-attended movie at the boxy old brick Lee Theater out on Williamson Road. Its three white letters spelling out its name above the marquee had to be the shortest name for any theater I'd ever seen. I didn't remember what movie was playing that night, but I remembered every touch of my arm around her shoulder, of her head leaning back and her dark hair brushing my cheek…

A lot happened after that. I wondered why we'd never talked of marriage. We were both young, we probably both thought there was plenty of time to think of things like that, we both had our own careers – at least until I derailed mine.

I looked at my watch. Time for the media guests' panel. I gathered up my tiny recorder, pocket tablet and pen, and set off for the Monroe Room downstairs where the actors were scheduled for an hour.

When I'd gone to some of the conventions during my first newspaper stint and written up articles on the various personalities attending, the panels always made it easy to get stories without even doing direct interviews. The audiences were always full of questions and, if nobody asked something I particularly wanted to know, I could always manage to throw that one in shortly before the panel ended. I figured it would be the same today.

And pretty much it was. It turned out that *The Planet Pawns* was a series based on the idea of a cosmic chess game, between two almost god-like alien creatures, with human space explorers filling the roles of pawns and other chess pieces. As the Knight, Luke Larabee had the ability to move with more flexibility than the other human pieces. As the Queen, Dana DuQueen was the most powerful piece on the interstellar board. In each episode, the human space voyagers on opposite sides didn't realize how they were being manipulated to make the moves they did against their antagonists. But in the story arc, they would gradually come to realize what was going on, and there might come a time when the pieces on the chessboard would rise up against the almost-omnipotent game players. Each week, the Larabee and DuQueen characters would learn a bit more about what was going on, and start to put together the scenario that the audience already fully understood.

It actually sounded kind of intriguing. I made a mental note to try and catch the next episode that came on. Chess was another thing that Cheyanne had taught me.

"I guess I got picked to play the Knight because I'd ridden so many horses in pictures," Larabee joked at one point. "It used to be that there were so many westerns that whole stables of horses were on hand to loan out to the studios. There were horses that could jump, horses that were trained to fall, and every actor had his favorite horse that the studio rented for him. Randolph Scott had Stardust. Jimmy Stewart had Pie. But the stables are long gone, now. If anyone wants to make a western anymore, the producer has to start with scratch, come up with his own horses, his own western sets, all that stuff that used to be universally available."

"The westerns were before my time," Dana commented, smiling prettily. "And probably before the time of most of you in this room." Larabee gave her a look, that made me wonder just how well these co-stars got along on their *Planet Pawns* set.

I was right, I didn't have to ask a single question. The two were more than happy to answer at length about their other work, how they got into the acting profession, and they told quite a few behind-the-camera jokes about what really went on during a shoot. It made for a cute little story, and it only took me about an hour to get it written up and sent to Bagley after I got back to my room.

I came back downstairs and went by the registration desk. The large schedule board with panels and speeches printed in blocks of time with variously-colored Magic Markers showed an obvious erasure where Chiswell's talk was to have been. Printed in its place was a more general talk on the subject of UFOs by three of the guest authors whose novels had sometimes touched on that theme. But Allgood's guest of honor speech was still scheduled for the 2 p.m. slot, and that was one I would have to make.

He was already being introduced, when I came into the lecture hall where the opening ceremonies had been held. The place was full. So I went down on aisle and squatted in a corner near the front with a few others who had come too late for seats. I looked around as much as I could in the crowd, but I probably couldn't have spotted Cheyanne even if she was somewhere in the hall.

Allgood nodded to the applause, as though accustomed to it, as he probably was. This time, the room was full of television cameras, both from local stations and the network and cable channels. Apparently they really expected Allgood to come up with something extraordinary.

The applause died down, and Allgood began to speak. No sooner had he uttered his first words than the start of a high-pitched sound caused everyone to cover their ears.

8—

Bill Ash as Air Force Captain: "Visits? That would indicate visitors." - Plan 9 from Outer Space, *1959*

"No!" I heard the word clearly, even over the awful sound. "No, damn it! Not again!"

I didn't realize at the time that it was me saying it.

If I'd stopped to think about what I was doing, I would never have done it. It was all pure adrenalin, pure instinct. I shoved my way through the crowd at the front that was now on its feet, and plunged through them toward where Allgood was standing, a look of frozen terror on his face.

"No," I heard him say, echoing my own reaction. "They promised…"

And then I crashed into him, wrapping my arms around his middle, toppling both of us toward the back of the raised stage and over its edge. We fell several feet, and the impact jarred me, but the hard floor would have been worse for Allgood who was underneath me.

I lay as flat as I could, head down. The screeching sound rose in volume, then I felt a kind of whump against the stage where I lay against its base.

Then everything got quiet again.

Hesitantly, I raised my head and peeked over the stage. The crowd of conventioneers milled around, looking stupefied. So did the television crews. I scrambled to my feet and helped Allgood to his. I stepped up onto the stage and, when I stepped onto the area where Allgood had been standing when I tackled him, I could feel a coldness seep right through my shoes into my feet.

I stepped away quickly, and looked down. Aside from a faint circular discoloration, there was nothing to indicate that part of the stage was any different from the rest of its surface.

Allgood had staggered up behind me. "I don't understand," he said. "They promised."

"They?" I said.

He shook his head. "It wasn't supposed to go this way."

"Doctor," I said, "I think you and I need to have a talk."

From what I'd seen of Allgood, he had seemed always to be a commanding figure, a take-charge guy who gave instructions rather than following them. But right now, he was so dazed that I think I could have told him to back creationism and he'd have done it.

I hustled him past the other occupants of the hall, including some TV stand-up broadcasters who wore fastidious attire above the belt – the part which would show on camera – and baggy jeans and tennis shoes below. They were still all too dazed to think of trying to grab him for an on-camera reaction, probably because none of them knew what had happened themselves.

I hustled him down the hall to the nearest elevator where, for once, there was no one waiting at all. "Do you have a car here?"

I had to repeat the question twice. "A rental," he finally responded.

"Where is it?"

"Outside. Down in the pay parking lot, back of the hotel."

"Keys?"

He reached into his pocket and handed me one, on a ring with a rental tag attached.

"Let's go."

I didn't know any more than the TV news crews or anyone else what had gone on back there, but I thought Allgood did. Before I cut loose from him, I was by-God going to find out what he knew, or thought he knew. And I thought somewhere away from the hotel was the place to do it. Maybe whatever was going on here wouldn't follow us.

Or maybe it would. But putting some distance between us and the source of whatever was happening seemed to me the way to bet.

Allgood seemed uncertain as to where his rental car was parked among the rows of vehicles in the outdoor lot. I started clicking the lock/unlock buttons on the key he'd handed me, and was soon rewarded by a beep and some lights flashing on and off. The rental was a maroon Subaru Outback. We got in.

The parking ticket was on the dash. I showed it to the attendant at the exit gate, paid the parking fee, and waited for the bar to raise in front of us before driving out of the hotel complex and onto Shenandoah Avenue. We hit Williamson Road, and turned onto Franklin until we hit First Street.

"Where are we going?" Allgood said. He seemed to be making a bit of a comeback.

"I don't know. Where do you think we'd be safest from whatever was back at the hotel?"

"Not inside," he said. "Nowhere inside a building. Somewhere outside."

"Okay." A few more twists and turns and I finally found a parking place. A short stroll put us on the Railwalk, where we continued onto the Martin Luther King Memorial Bridge, which I remembered as the First Street Bridge from when I'd been in Roanoke before. A larger-than-life bronze statue of King looked over us, as we sat ourselves on one of the benches around it.

"All right, Doctor," I said. "Give."

He looked directly at me for the first time. "Who the hell are you?" he said.

"My name's Simon Carr. More to the point, I'm the guy who just kept you from being frozen or whatever it is that blue ray does to people. I know a little bit about what's going on, probably just enough to be dangerous. But, so help me, before I get up from this bench, I'm going to know a hell of a lot more."

"Why should I talk to you?" he asked, reaching the stage of mild irritation for the first time. He was starting to regain his composure, so I tried to think of a way to keep him off-balance for a bit longer.

"Cheyanne Caday knows me," I said. "I believe she would vouch for me."

"You know Cheyanne?" he said, sounding a little surprised.

"Think about it, Doctor. If you keep this entirely to yourself, they can assure themselves of secrecy by incapacitating or eliminating you. If you tell me, they'd have no reason to do any of that."

"Unless they took care of you, too," he said. "Have you thought about that, Mr. Carr?"

I had, indeed. What was I doing, mixing it this whatever-it-was, anyway? I didn't have a dog in this fight. Even if I knew everything that was going on, what was I going to do about it? I was a humble scribe, not someone with any authority.

But I had probably invited myself in when I got Allgood out of harm's way in the past fifteen minutes – although it seemed a lot longer ago than that. I might already be a marked man. If so, it behooved me to know what I was up against.

"I've seen my share of strange stuff," I assured him

"Nothing as strange as this," he said. "But I may as well tell you, I suppose. I doubt if you will believe any of it."

"What, are you taking a page out of Chiswell's book, now? Are you going to tell me we have an alien visitor or something hanging around?"

He looked me right in the eye. "Yes, that's exactly what I'm going to tell you," he said. "For starters."

9—

Walter Sande as Admiral Carey: "I wonder what kind of world we're opening the door on?" - Red Planet Mars, *1952*

Passers-by walked back and forth across the bridge as we sat there, him talking, me listening, and them having no idea how what was passing between this could affect them. I guess it could have affected all of us, by which I mean the whole human race.

"It started in the middle of the last century," he said. He gestured toward the artificial star, un-illuminated now off in the distance to the south. "Right up there on Mill Mountain."

That was what Allgood referred to as "the first landing," the original visitors from somewhere out there to our world.

Earth had been a long-time object of curiosity to others out there, because it teemed with so many and such different forms of life – a number less than when the varied life-forms were at their height, of course, because humankind had managed to drive some of them to extinction. But apparently there were relatively few among other inhabited worlds in contact with one another where life had gone through the kind of evolutionary process that ours had. It was one of a kind, at least among the planets that any of them had visited so far, a jewel of the galaxy.

But its most advanced life-forms threatened to destroy all that. The threat had taken many forms in more recent decades – hunting creatures to extinction, development of biological weapons of war, environmental abuses, nuclear missiles, and probably more to come.

That first landing had been in defiance of a kind of cosmic quarantine that outsiders had imposed on our Earth. It wasn't a quarantine which was official in any way – the various creatures from other planets had civilizations and customs so wildly different that the concept of treaties or political agreements was futile – but it had been something of a common understanding. And the first visitors had broken it.

Their motives had been pure. They had sent a few emissaries that had volunteered to take our forms – yes, these particular beings could do that quite readily – and observe firsthand what motivated our seemingly destructive impulses. Perhaps something could be done about them.

"That first landing let the genie out of the lamp," Allgood said. "Within a few years, there were representatives of at least two other alien cultures at large on our Earth. They continued to make their clandestine landings somewhere on Mill Mountain. Their various types of landing craft were small enough to escape notice up there."

"Does all this confirm that portion of UFO sightings that we've never been able to explain satisfactorily? Was Professor Chiswell right all the time?" I asked.

Allgood gave a short laugh. "UFOs are, by definition, unidentified flying objects. If you identify one – if you find it's a balloon, or an aircraft, or the planet Venus, whatever – well, then, it's no longer unidentified, is it?"

"There was a UFO flap back around 1990 about 80 miles west of here. People living in a town named Wytheville were seeing all kinds of exotic lights in the sky for maybe a month. Even back then, I imagine Chiswell might have been among all the UFO buffs who descended on that place, looking for what they could see. A few of the accounts made it into the Roanoke paper."

"I remember that. I don't know what those were. Maybe the defense department was testing something. Or maybe it was the real thing. Well, the real unidentified thing, I mean."

"Fair enough. Okay, we have two or three sets of aliens matriculating on Earth, and they all have ways of looking like us. What are they doing here?"

"That's the real question, isn't it? The ones from the first landing seem pretty benign. They are only seeking ways to keep us from wiping out the flora and fauna and diversity of animal life that makes this world so unique."

"Then they aren't the ones going around zapping people with death rays or whatever," I heard myself saying, and was momentarily amazed that I was accepting all this from Allgood so calmly. And maybe gullibly? Was I really sitting here, on a bench along the Martin Luther King Memorial Bridge, swallowing all this about aliens among us?

I guess, yes, I was.

"No, they aren't the ones," Allgood said. "I don't know much about the ones who are doing that."

"Well, that's the big question, isn't it? How do you know about any of this at all?"

He looked startled. "Don't you know that already? I thought you said you knew…" He stopped.

"I said I'd seen my share of stuff that couldn't be explained," I said. "Although I'm sure most of it had a conventional explanation. It's just that nobody had figured it out yet."

"Then you…" He stopped again, and seemed to be gathering himself. "Do you actually believe anything I've told you?"

"I've been wondering about that, myself. And, you know, the strangest thing is that – well, yes. I do."

He began looking at me warily, edging away just a bit. "You're not – you're not one of them, are you? Testing me? To see if I would keep my word to stay quiet about all this?"

I couldn't help smiling. "No, Doctor. This is not a test. I'm as human as you are." And then, another thought struck me. "You *are*, aren't you?"

"All too human, I'm afraid. Yes. All right, we say we're both human. I've been telling you things about which I swore to remain silent. You say they are all news to you. Why do you want to know something which could be so dangerous to you?"

"We already covered that. I'm human. But you still haven't answered my question. How do *you* know about all this that you're telling me?"

"How else?" he said. "They told me. Or one of them did."

10–

Paul Christian as Professor Tom Nesbitt: "The world's been here for millions of years. Man's been walking upright for a comparatively short time. Mentally we're still crawling."
- The Beast from 20,000 Fathoms, *1953*

"Who told you?" I demanded.

"I'm afraid the human identity of that individual is one secret I must keep from you, Mr. Carr," Allgood said. "In any case, it's the ones we don't know about that are the danger to us. To you, too, now that you know what I know."

"Yeah," I shook my head. "Kind of lonely, isn't it?" Then another thought struck me. "Is this the big announcement you were going to make at your big StarCon speech? The one that had all the TV reporters on hand?"

"I was not going to say quite everything that I've told you. Nothing about the second or possible third wave of aliens. I was just going to talk about those from the first landing – with their permission. Or at least with the permission of one of them. And that one may be the only one left, although I've never been told that is the case."

"What happened to the others?"

"I don't know. I'm not sure anything happened to them. But from a few hints in conversations where things have been let drop… Well, we've been talking about how deadly a world this can be for life forms of all kinds, haven't we?"

"Did you think anyone would believe you? I mean, making this kind of claim in the middle of a science fiction convention, of all places…"

"No, I didn't expect many people to believe me. That's one reason why we chose this venue, so that it wouldn't become a major cultural shock to civilization. Think of the effect that acceptance of my claim would have on organized religion, on cosmology, on our tendency to fear or hate what we do not understand. Coming out this way, it would be a national amusement for a time, something for the late night talk show hosts to joke about. But gradually, very gradually, the people who make policy atop our various nations would begin having second thoughts, as what I would have said began fitting into scenarios that they knew and understood. It would happen by such small degrees that the impact would be minimized. People would have time to get used to it. True, I was risking a loss of credibility myself, which could have had an ill effect on my book sales, or my being invited to those same talk shows, but then…"

I nodded. "It could also have had the opposite effect. I mean, supermarket tabloids sell pretty well. You could have become a hot commodity."

"I thought of that."

I was sure he had. "All right. So what do you plan to do now? Go back and try again at StarCon? Whoever promised to protect you obviously isn't doing a very good job."

"No," he agreed. "And that was quite a shock to me."

"What about Chiswell? Was he going to make the same announcement, or some variation of it?"

"I don't really know. Perhaps those others were hedging their bets, so to speak. I really did think that Chiswell had staged all that last night, you know. The man is a bigger publicity seeker than von Daniken ever thought of being."

"What do you think now?" I asked.

"I think he was a victim of the same phenomenon from which you saved me."

We both sat and thought about that for a while. "But wait, what about the first victim? The kid who was just a sci-fi fan? Why would they have hit him with that whatever it is?"

"I cannot imagine. It make no sense."

"Maybe he saw something? Stumbled onto something?" My cell phone vibrated against my hip in its belt holster. "Just a minute." I opened it up and saw who was calling: Bagley.

"What the hell happened over there this morning? Why haven't you checked in? Why don't we have the story? Why didn't you update me?"

"Hello? Who is this?" I asked innocently.

"You know damned well who this is, you sonuvabitch! There's stuff all over the television news shows, but nobody knows what the hell to make of it. It looked like Allgood was about to say whatever he was going to say, and some idiot came running up after him onto the stage and took him down. Now, Allgood's gone, the crazy guy's gone, and everybody's in an uproar."

"I'm sitting next to Doctor Allgood right now," I told him.

"You're what? How did you... Oh, no! Not again."

"Yep, that's right. I'm a participant in the story again. Do you still want me to write it?"

"I thought that idiot looked familiar, even from the back! Simon, what the blazes is going on? I'm trying to cover your ass, but I'm working in the dark here."

"I could give you the story right now," I said. "But you wouldn't print it. Not without some kind of confirmation."

"Story?" Allgood was showing a sudden interest in my conversation with Bagley. "Are you a reporter?"

"How do you know what I'd print?" Bagley demanded. "It couldn't be any crazier than all the stuff that's being spouted on all the channels right now."

"Give me that key," Allgood said, reaching right into my trousers pocket and grabbing it. Then he was on his feet and walking quickly in the direction where we'd left his rental.

"Hey, don't go away," I called after him.

"I'm not going anywhere, dammit!" Bagley's voice came over the cell.

"Not you," I said, halfway starting after Allgood's retreating figure. "Oh, well, he's gone now."

"Who's gone?"

"Allgood. He didn't approve of me talking to someone like you."

"Look here, Simon..."

"Bagley, listen to me. I've got the story, I know what Allgood was planning to say in his big announcement, but it's so far out that we might be a laughingstock if we print it. I'll get it emailed to you in plenty of time for tonight's first-run deadline, and you can decide whether you really want it in the morning paper."

"Morning paper? You're even more old school than I am. We want it on twitter, on Facebook, on our blogs, on our on-line updates…"

"Believe me, all that would make the whole thing more confusing than it already is. I might have been able to get some confirmation from Professor Chiswell, if he could talk, if anybody would believe him."

"Chiswell? He can talk. He and the kid have about recovered from whatever ailed them. In fact, the boy apparently left the hospital on his own this morning. Got his doc's permission to check out. Chiswell's still there, but he might be well enough to get out today, too."

"Chiswell's lucid? And he's still at the hospital?"

"He was, last time anybody here checked. Why?"

Before I clicked off, I said, "I'm on my way."

11—

Hayden Roarke as Doctor Bronson: "If our calculations prove to be correct, this will be the most frightening discovery of all time."
- When Worlds Collide, *1952*

Using my phone's AroundMe app to locate a taxi, I waited back on First Street for my pickup and headed to Roanoke Community Hospital. I only hoped I'd be in time to catch Chiswell – and that I could get in to see him. Soon we were heading south on U.S. 220, and soon we'd arrived at the 10-floor hospital building, backed up against what looked like a small mountain.

And a little farther off, I noticed I could see Mill Mountain.

I didn't know where to start looking for Chiswell in this sprawling complex, with its hundreds of beds, but I finally located an information desk where a helpful lady checked on his status, said he was still a patient but would probably check out soon, and gave me directions and a room number.

The door was closed. I knocked, and heard a feeble, "Yes, come on in."

Chiswell was up, and dressed, apparently wearing the same sweater as yesterday. "Oh, I thought you were one of the nurses," he said. "Can I do something for you?"

"I'm hoping I can do something for you, Professor," I said. I gave him an abbreviated rundown of who I was, glossing over my temporary relationship with *The Roanoke Times* and letting him know I'd had a long talk with Doctor Allgood. He had been making noises about being anxious to get back to StarCon but, when he heard I'd elicited some new information from Allgood, he seemed willing to spend a little more time with me.

We went through the checkout procedure. I told him that I'd get a cab to take us back to the convention hotel. I suggested that we find a place for coffee or a sandwich and talk a bit first and, after a brief hesitation, he agreed.

The ground floor refreshment facility was named Java the Hutt, which we both thought appropriate in light of the theme of the weekend. We both had some of their specialty coffee, and Chiswell asked me what Allgood had said to me.

I took a deep breath, and told him. I also told him what I had told Allgood, about my being a sort of insurance policy for him if he gave me his version of events and they were hazardous to his health.

When I was through, he didn't react for a few minutes. He sipped his coffee, put down the cup, and turned his sleepy eyes on me.

"Did you believe what the good doctor told you?" he asked.

Now it was my turn to hesitate, but finally I nodded. "I did."

"Would you have believed me, if I had told you such a story?"

"Maybe not, at first. You do have a reputation of embellishing things, Professor."

"You are honest, at least. Very well, I will tell you my story. And I will not, as you say, embellish it. You may then take it or leave it."

I leaned forward. "Fair enough," I said.

"I suppose you know all about 'flying saucers,' the name given these disc-shaped craft by some anonymous headline writer after Kenneth Arnold's first sighting of nine such objects when he was flying near Mount Rainier in Washington state. Almost overnight, people started seeing these objects all over the country, and many jumped to the conclusion that they were extraterrestrial in origin."

I had activated my little recorder, having put a fresh cassette in it that morning. "Why do you think that was?" I asked.

"I believe there were two reasons. One, none of our airplanes resembled flying discs so, if they were real, they were from somewhere else. Two, I do not suppose you are old enough to have read the old pulp magazines, the ones with garish colors usually showing a scantily-clad woman being pursued by a bug-eyed monster?"

"I've seen some old copies," I said.

"Then you may already realize that those pulp artists often depicted alien spacecraft on the covers as circular in shape. I suppose they were looking for some alternative to our own rocket-shaped designs. So my contention is that we were already conditioned to believe that disc-shaped objects had to come from outer space."

I hadn't thought of it that way. But, now that I recalled some of those covers, he was right. There had been flying saucers all over those magazines before anybody came up for that name for them.

"Now, I am not saying that all those artists had entered into a conspiracy to prepare us for flying saucer sightings," Chiswell said. "But that was the effect. And the movies that came along in the wake of those sightings only reinforced the supposition."

"So you think science fiction played a role in propagating the craze?" I asked.

"Absolutely! Why, the editor of *Amazing Stories*, the first science fiction magazine ever published, actually hired Mister Arnold to go interview others who had reported sightings, and published the result in his magazine, no doubt sensationalizing them to some extent. Now, the first movie to capitalize on the sightings, a low-budget thing unimaginatively titled *The Flying Saucer*, came out in 1950 gave it an Earth-bound explanation, having it invented by an American scientist and spies from various countries trying to steal it."

"So there was only one saucer in that version."

"Correct. But after that, the floodgates opened. Hollywood grabbed up science fictional literary properties and added flying saucers to them. John Campbell's story, "Who Goes There?", became *The Thing*, which arrived in a flying saucer. Harry Bates' "Farewell to the Master" became *The Day the Earth Stood Still*, which started with the arrival of a flying saucer in Washington, D.C. Raymond Jones' series of stories compiled as *This Island, Earth*, had a flying saucer added in the screen version. And on, and on."

"I seem to remember that even the *Invaders from Mars* arrived in a flying saucer."

"Indeed, that was the spacecraft of choice. And we had our own P. T. Barnums out there proving, indeed, that there is a sucker born every minute. We had contactees meeting with saucer pilots from Venus – we were less aware of conditions on our 'sister planet' at the time – and places like the planet Clarion, wherever that was. In fact, the author who wrote about going out in the desert at night to meet with the beautiful female pilot was eventually divorced by his wife. And she named Captain Aura Rhanes from Clarion as co-respondent."

"You've got to be kidding me."

"So you see, Mr. Carr, flying saucers have influenced events upon our own world even if they never existed. Pilots have died chasing what they thought were flying saucers, but which were probably natural phenomena that they misinterpreted. The bright planet Venus, for example."

"All this is fascinating, Professor. But what's it got to do with you being here in Roanoke right now?"

"I merely wanted you to have the background. Flying saucers became jokes, pop culture icons, the subject of ridicule. But there was always that small percentage of sightings that no one could ever explain. The ones down the road from us in Wytheville a few decades ago have never been explained."

"I wondered if you'd looked into those."

"I have looked into many such incidents, and made a good living writing books about some of them. As I noted, whatever the public believes about flying saucers – and a surprising number do believe they are real, according to various surveys – they nearly always sell. Perhaps my approach was seen as more credible than many such authors or consultants."

And then he dropped his little bomb so casually that it

didn't hit me for several seconds. "At least I believed that was why they chose to contact me."

12—

Robert Cornthwaite as Doctor Carrington: "We're getting nowhere."

Douglas Spencer as "Scotty": "We're consistent!"
- The Thing (from Another World) *1951*

I was riding in still another cab, heading back up U.S. 220 escorting Professor Chiswell back to the hotel. I had no idea what he was going to do when he got there, but he certainly seemed to be recovered from his ordeal.

His tale had not been that much different from the one Doctor Allgood had told me, except Chiswell seemed to have been in touch with a more nasty breed of alien. He claimed he was told that his more objective approach to the UFO investigations lent too much credence to his conclusions, and that he might be dangerous to their presence on our world. Also like Allgood, he wouldn't tell me the identity of the alien who had threatened him. "I've told you too much already," he had said. "But your insurance policy argument was rather persuasive."

StarCon was still in full swing, somewhat to my surprise. With all that had happened, I wondered if there had been consideration given to canceling it altogether. Apparently not, though. It seemed that nothing was going to be allowed to stand in the way of sci-fi fans and their passion.

I had halfway decided to give Bagley a rebate on the amount in the contract he'd faxed me before I came down here. I'd given him one story on a TV series that anyone on the paper's arts and entertainment staff could have done as well – assuming they'd gotten to interview the actors, of course – and a half-assed story about one guest of honor being hospitalized with only the vaguest of explanations.

There was still one more story I could give him, and that was the one Allgood and Chiswell had told me. Or gotten me involved in, I should say, because now I was as much a threat to their alien contactees as they ever were. That was a motivation, of sorts, to get the damned thing into print, so it would no longer be my exclusive secret. However, the decision to print it or not would not be mine. After my earlier phone conversation with Bagley, I wasn't sure how much credibility I still had with him.

But the story behind what the two scientist/showmen were going to say at this Star City convention was what Bagley had hired me to get for him. I guessed I was obligated, legally and morally, to produce.

Once again, I sat before the desk in my hotel room and booted up my laptop. It was late afternoon by now, and I needed to concentrate to get something coherent together, especially considering the subject matter. Nothing like having to produce an article as complicated as this one would be on deadline, I thought. Sort of like trying to write a 30,000-word novel in 48 hours, or something equally insane. But nobody ever claimed that journalists were a particularly sane breed.

Well, as a Chinese sage once said, the journey of a million miles begins with a single step. I started pecking away at the little keyboard, wishing I'd brought along my full-size plug-in from my home-office in Highland Falls to use instead.

I tried to make both of my subjects sound credible, which was not easy considering the subject matter. I had not been as up front as I should with Allgood, and I would like to have gotten his blessing on the piece as I had with Chiswell. But in the end, he had found out what I was doing, and he left without trying to talk me out of doing it. Both men seemed more than ready to accept the insurance argument I'd given them. I just hoped that I wouldn't be the one who would have to pay off in the end.

It may have been because the whole affair seemed so unlikely that I wasn't all that fearful for my own safety. After all, even the boy and the man who had been struck down had both recovered, and in a short time, too. Maybe the alien who was behind those attempts – I was still amused by how easily my acceptance of the word and meaning behind "alien" was coming by now – had only been trying to incapacitate the targets, not kill them. I still had no idea why he, or it, had made an attack on the kid. If Jimmy Cox had returned to StarCon, I probably needed to seek him out and get his story, too, assuming I could find him in this crowd.

I knew Bagley and others at the paper would be going over this story with a fine-tooth comb, even if they finally decided to go with it. So I was extremely careful with my phraseology, and that required more time than a story of its length would normally have taken. The approach I was trying for was basic down to earth, no pun intended. The reader could believe what the main two subjects of the story had to say, or could decide, to quote a character from one of my favorite '50s SF flying saucer movies, that they were "stuffed absolutely clean full of wild blueberry muffins." Even when I saw *The Thing* as a kid, the character with whom I identified was the newspaper reporter. And here I was, like him, telling people the equivalent of his "Watch the skies! Keep watching the skies!"

I also did something I had never done in any article that I had ever written: I put myself in it. "Disclaimer," I wrote. "I was the one who tackled Allgood when I thought he was in the same danger that Professor Chiswell had been." And then I went on to spell out why I'd felt that way based on what I'd seen before. I hadn't seen any of the television coverage of that day's debacle, so I didn't know how much, if any, of that strange blue ray would show up on any of their recording devices. There was no way that piercing sound which always seemed to precede it could be missed, though. Maybe that would add credence to what I was writing.

By the time I finished, I was covered with perspiration, and not because the room lacked air-conditioning. It had been more of an effort than I'd realized. I leaned back, and realized I was hungry. I called room service, and decided on the New York strip with potato and spinach from the Regency Room. While I waited, I went through the finished story once more, made a couple of minor changes, typed in Bagley's email address and sent the story attachment off into the ether.

I expected my room phone or my cell to go off any second, but nothing happened. Maybe Bagley was having dinner, too. Maybe I should call the newsroom and let somebody know the story had been sent. Maybe…

There was a knock at the door.

Well, I thought, that was fast. But I was hungry, so I hurried to the door and pulled it open.

It wasn't room service. It was Delaney, the investigator from the Roanoke Police Department. And he didn't look happy.

13—

Michael Rennie as Klaatu: "We have come to visit you in peace, and with good will." - The Day the Earth Stood Still, *1951*

We stood looking at one another for what seemed like a full minute, before I stepped aside and silently ushered him in.

"Don't get all worried on me, Mr. Carr," Delaney said as, uninvited, he ambled over to my laptop and looked at what was on the screen. "I'm calling on you in entirely amicable fashion."

"Okay," I said. "Have a seat." I put myself in the chair by the computer, forcing him to take the chair away from it. Not that he probably hadn't already figured out what I'd been doing.

"You'll be glad to know that I got the cover from your bed back to the hotel, I guess. You won't have to pay whatever it cost for using it to wrap up that kid yesterday."

"Thanks. But did you come up here just to tell me that?"

"You keep popping up in the middle of whatever's going on here, Mr. Carr," he said, easing his bulk into the other chair. "If I had any idea what it was, I might think you were causing it."

"I assure you, I'm not causing anything."

"Well, things sure do have a way of happening around you, then," he said. "That was you on TV this evening, wasn't it? Taking down one of the major guest stars as this sci-fi convention?"

"What else did you see in that TV bit?" I asked. I was genuinely curious.

"I saw the scientist, astronomer, whatever he is, walk out onto the stage and start to speak. I saw people all of a sudden jumping around and clapping their hands over their ears. I heard a noise, but it didn't seem bad enough to cause all that melee."

"Probably the TV recording equipment couldn't do full justice to it," I said. "You'd have been covering your ears, too."

"Reasonable, I guess. The next thing I saw was you barreling through the crowd like a Virginia Tech fullback and taking down the would-be speaker. The two of you disappeared over the back end of the stage, and then the camera cut away."

"You didn't see anything else on the stage, right after we tumbled behind it?"

"Funny you should ask," he said. "Yeah, there was something – like the beam of a searchlight, but not anywhere near as bright. One second it was there, right where the two of you had been, and the next second it was gone."

There was another knock at the door.

"I ordered something to eat," I said. "I'm starved. Can I

get something for you?"

"Naw, I've eaten. But don't let me keep you."

I went to the door, got my supper, tipped the delivery guy, and started to return to my seat. Then I had another idea.

"Okay, Mr. Delaney. Let's switch places. I'll eat, and you scroll through what's on that computer. It may answer every question you've got. If it doesn't, I'll try to answer them myself."

"Thanks." He got up. "I was kind of hoping you'd give me a look. The little bit I saw when I first came in was mighty intriguing."

"Help yourself," I said, and we switched. The steak was good, and I gave it my undivided attention for the next fifteen minutes.

Delaney took his time reading the piece. I began to feel defensive, like when an editor was going through something I'd written with such careful deliberation that I knew he'd find something to complain about. I kept telling myself that Delaney wasn't an editor, and he wasn't able to change stuff on me, anyway. The story had already been received – assuming Bagley had gotten back to the newsroom and had looked at his computer's in-box.

Nevertheless, a reporter can't help taking a little pride in what he writes, and I found myself a tad anxiously waiting for Delaney's reaction. Maybe it would give me a clue as to how other readers would react to it, assuming that it got into print.

Finally, he pushed his chair back from the desk and rubbed at his eyes. "Is this for real?" he asked. "You're not writing something for one of those sci-fi magazines?"

"It's for real. Believe it or not."

He turned the chair around so he was facing me. "So you're saying we got space aliens living among us, disguised to look just like we do, and some of them are good aliens, and some may be not so good, and they told you all this, and we're all supposed to believe it?"

"All of that's correct. Except the aliens didn't tell me. They told the other two guys."

"Right. These are aliens, in human form, and they told Allgood and Chiswell they weren't really human, appearances to the contrary, but were creatures from other worlds pretending to be human. And Allgood and Chiswell believed them, even though they looked human, spoke English, didn't have their fishbowl helmets with them, just based on their word that they were not of this Earth. Absolutely. Why wouldn't anybody buy a story like that?"

"I don't know how the aliens convinced them that all this was the truth," I said. I had to admit that Delaney had a point, because neither Chiswell or Allgood would go beyond a certain point in either of their accounts that they gave me. "But both of them seemed utterly persuaded."

"You don't think these two publicity hogs might have gotten together, and said, hey, let's see how far we can string along this reporter, make up this crazy tale and see if he'll buy it, see if he'll even put it in the paper? It would be a hell of a lot easier to believe something like that than what you've written here," he said, gesturing at the laptop.

"Yeah, I can see how you'd think that," I said, and wondered if Bagley and others in the newsroom were having similar thoughts. "But what about all that strange stuff that's been happening to people at this convention?"

"What about it? You said yourself, in that story, you described the sound as being like feedback from a microphone. It wouldn't be hard for someone to produce something like that. And a blue ray? Anyone with a powerful flashlight and a bluish lens cover could do that."

"But the effects of it…" I began.

"You haven't been paying attention to the costumers at this convention," Delaney said. "Don't all those Klingons look just as real as the ones on the big screen? And the Storm Troopers? Don't all those Spock ears look natural on the people wearing them? Didn't that green girl in the bikini look like she was green from head to toe? Hell, man, the art of makeup has gotten as good for amateurs as it ever was in the movies. If you can make someone look like a zombie or a werewolf right here at this hotel, you can sure stick enough stuff on someone's face to make it look like he's been hit by something weird."

"Yeah, but…" I trailed off. He was actually making pretty some good points. Had I really been merely a gullible newshound that the two perennial TV talking heads were having fun with, or maybe were using to enhance their talk show credentials? "But the Cox boy and Chiswell had something happen to them. The doctor sent them to the hospital."

"Who was that doctor, by the way? He turned up mighty conveniently, didn't he? Do you remember his name?"

"His name…" I had never heard it. I just assumed that the hotel people had found him among the guests, or maybe he was close by somewhere and available. "But the hospital people wouldn't have been fooled, would they?"

"I don't know. But those two made an awful quick recovery after being hospitalized, wouldn't you say? I haven't seen anything more of the kid, but Chiswell certainly shows no lasting effects."

My discomfort began to increase. "Maybe I should call my editor. Maybe we should hold onto the story a little longer…"

"Yeah. Maybe you should. Better safe than sorry, and all that. But it's up to you. No skin off my nose. I'm just surprised that a big city writer could be so easily taken in."

I stopped, with my hand on the phone. "Big city writer?

Where are you getting that?"

"Well, not far from New York City, anyway. That's big city enough for me."

"But how do you know where I live? Have you been investigating me, Mr. Delaney?"

"I got ears. I listen to what people say. I heard someone say where you were from."

"How long have you been with the Roanoke department, Mr. Delaney? Did you grow up here, too?"

"What's my time with the department got to do with all this?"

"It just occurred to me to wonder. After all, neither one of our star celebrities told me what identity had been assumed by his resident alien. It might even be that of a police investigator."

Delaney stood up, and unbuttoned his coat. "Now you're really going off the deep end," he said.

He pushed his coat back, and I could see the holstered pistol on his hip.

14—

Steve Pendleton as FBI Agent Briggs: "Did you ever stop to think that perhaps this Doctor Martin isn't really THE Doctor Martin?" - Killers from Space, *1954*

The phone rang.

We stood there, looking at one another. The phone continued to ring. Delaney let the flap of his coat fall forward again, and stepped back. "Don't you think you ought to answer that?"

I kept my eye on him, but picked up the receiver. "Hello?"

"Simon!" It was Bagley's voice. "Have you gone off the deep end?"

I couldn't help chuckling. "You're the second person to

suggest that in the last thirty seconds."

"I just got through reading this. Will these two birds deny telling you what you've written if it appears in print?"

"I've got them both on tape," I said.

"Did they know you were taping them?"

"No, but Virginia law hasn't changed, has it? As long as one party to the conversation knows a recording is being made…"

"Okay, all right, so we can prove they said what you say they said. But – Simon, aliens among us? Really?"

"You hired me to cover what they were going to say at this convention, when they barred the print press. Well, this is what they were going to say, even if they never got to say it. I wouldn't blame you if you decided not to print it, but this is what you said you wanted me to get."

"I'm going to have to think about this," Bagley said. "I feel like somebody's been pounding my head with railroad tie, a skillet or a paving brick."

"Well, it wasn't me," I said. "By the way, did you ever find out why they wouldn't let any print reporters into this convention?"

"Yeah. Some of the people who'd worked on some other sci-fi conventions got P.O.-ed at us because they didn't think we gave their events enough coverage. So they decided, to hell with us, they just wouldn't let us in at all. Especially now that there were some high-profile speakers that we might actually want to cover."

"Is that all?"

"Apparently so. Makes you wonder, doesn't it? Makes me wonder why I talked the powers-that-be into approving so much expense money to get you in there, when I didn't think it was really that big a deal in the first place. Tell someone they can't have something, and they want it. I guess I'm not immune, myself."

"We'll talk about the expenses before I leave," I told him. "I don't think three stories – or two, if you don't use the one you've got – really justify what you offered. We can negotiate."

"Yeah, let's do that, so at least I'll lay eyes on you before you go back. Do you realize I haven't seen you since you got here?"

After I hung up, I noticed Delaney actually had a small grin on his face. "What's so funny?" I asked.

"I thought you'd about decided that I was an alien in disguise, and were about to jump me. That's why I displayed the artillery."

"And I thought you might be an alien who wanted to talk me out of exposing this stuff," I said. "And I still don't know why you've gone to all the trouble of researching me."

"Hell, maybe we're both aliens. Maybe everybody on Earth is. Wasn't there something a few years ago about a rock from Mars found in Antarctica that made some of the NASA folks think maybe microbes from Mars seeded life here 'way back' when? And that we were all actually Martians?"

"Yeah, but I think that got discredited the way my piece for the paper might be. If it was true, though, it would mean Bradbury was right. He said in the last chapter of *The Martian Chronicles* that we were all Martians. Of course, it was a little more involved than just that…"

"Spare me." Delaney held up a hand. "In case you hadn't guessed, I'm not a sci-fi buff. I've seen enough movies to know what a Klingon is supposed to be, but that's about it. And for your information, I still have my doubts about that story you've apparently filed. But I guess you know what you're doing."

He turned toward the door, but stopped. "Oh! And the reason I looked into you, I thought you might be some kind of agitator bent on making trouble, especially after your little act in the lecture hall with Doctor Allgood. There are trouble makers like that all over the place, these days. But I guess you're just what you say you are."

"Whatever that is." I stacked my dishes and looked at my watch. "You know, I haven't gotten to check out the dealers' room at this con yet. I might want to do that before it closes for the evening, in half an hour. Want me to look for any sci-fi knickknacks for you?"

"Yeah. Get me one of those blue-ray freeze guns. Or maybe an alien detector, so I can tell whether someone is really who he says he is. Goodnight." And he was gone.

There had been a time when I could always find a used SF paperback I'd never read, from back in the days when that sense of wonder I liked still permeated the stories. But the only books I saw as I made my way up and down the aisles between the dealers' tables were either for gaming, or were print-on-demand copies being sold by authors I didn't know. There were a few boxes of DVDs, but nothing I couldn't live without – some SF, some fantasy, some horror, some martial arts, some anime, a good variety of stuff but nothing that particularly appealed. There was jewelry, unicorn earrings and Saturn necklaces among the pieces. Some StarCon T-shirts, with a picture of a sword-wielding woman warrior reproduced from a drawing by one of the guest artists. There were buttons with some funny sayings on them, which tempted me as much as anything I'd seen so far. No pulp magazines, not even any comic books. I guessed I was just out of touch with today's SF interests.

I thought again that maybe I'd let Bagley bring me here under false pretenses.

I was about to leave when I spotted the Cox boy. I almost didn't recognize him, without an expression of horror on his face. It was his stringy blond hair sticking out on all sides that gave him away. He was staring at a table with photos of Dana DuQueen in various exotic poses, but at this hour she wasn't on hand to autograph them. There were also photos of Luke Larabee, but he wasn't looking at those. A normal red-blooded American male, I decided, with all his priorities in the right place.

I made my way over to where he was standing, thinking that I'd identify myself as one of the people he encountered on the elevator yesterday and see how he was doing. I might even get something out of him as to how he'd come to be in that condition, and maybe what the condition even was.

He glanced my way, and seemed suddenly to decide he had urgent business elsewhere. He went striding off in the direction opposite the way I was approaching. Well, it was probably too late for me to recall my article, even if he did have something to add to it. But it would be really interesting to find out what role he played in all that had been going on since yesterday.

Hell, I *needed* to find out. I started off after him. He glanced over his shoulder, and increased his pace until he reached the door to the hallway.

Then he began to sprint.

15—

Duke Moore as Lieutenant Harper: "Kelton, get down there and check it out."

Paul Marco as Patrolman Kelton: "Well, how do I do that, sir?"

Harper: "By going down there and checking it out!"
- Plan 9 from Outer Space, *1959*

The kid was fast. But the hallway was crowded, and he couldn't make the progress he might have made in a less congested area.

"Hey, Jimmy," I called from behind him. "Hold up a minute."

He stopped, and turned toward me. "Who are you? What do you want?"

"Nothing. I just wanted to ask how you were since you got out of the hospital," I said.

"Hey, I remember you. You were one of the three guys in the elevator."

"That's right. What in the world had happened to you?"

"I don't know." His eyes shifted. "I can't remember what happened. It's all a blank to me."

That was disappointing, but I had no reason to doubt him. Except… "But you remembered me," I said.

"Yeah, vaguely, kind of," he said. "Well…" He started to move off.

"Those were nice pictures of The Queen from *Planet Pawns*," I said, in an attempt to keep him talking a little longer. "You know, there's going to be an article in the paper tomorrow on her and Luke. You might enjoy it."

"Yeah. I'll have to get a copy. Well, see you around."

So much for my gift of gab, I thought. I used to be pretty fair at putting people at ease when I wanted to talk to them. Maybe I was slipping. Or maybe he was just an ungrateful young knuckle-dragger.

I followed Jimmy out of the dealers' room, and past several tables of gamers involved in competitions I didn't understand. "Hey, look," I heard someone call from the direction of the lobby. "We're on television!"

A half-dozen young people crowded around the lobby's big-screen TV, where the footage focused predictably on the most outlandish costumes, some of which would no doubt show up in the traditional con costume competition that was probably coming up soon. A couple of remote-controlled R2-D2s went rolling by on the screen, not to mention a hulking Darth Vader.

Then the coverage switched to that afternoon's appearance by Doctor Allgood. I heard the high-pitched sound, although muted somewhat by the TV recording devices, and saw myself go running onto the stage and pulling Allgood down behind it. I looked for the blue ray of light and thought I spotted it, but I may have imagined it. The reporter doing the voice-over made some comment about some unscheduled excitement as apparently some anonymous critic of the guest speaker got carried away, and added that no charges had been filed in the matter.

"What was that?" one onlooker said. "I missed it, I was watching the sword defense demonstrations by the Society for Creative Anachronism folks."

"Nobody knows," he was told. "But Allgood never did get to make that speech and the revelations we'd all been hearing about. Probably it was some kind of put-on."

That was the end of it. My little foray into the news hadn't made any waves, not with this group. Well, that was all right.

I stopped by the registration desk to see if there had been anything added to the programming on the Magic Marker schedule. The art room was closed for the evening. I'd have to stop by there tomorrow. The guest artists would have pieces there, and even the amateurs who attended these cons often had good stuff. There were still a few panel discussions still coming up tonight and, sure enough, there was the costume contest where people I'd been seeing in various guises over the past two days would compete for top prizes in various categories. I decided to go sit in on that for a while.

Just as I remembered from long-ago cons, I was still in awe at the amount of work that had obviously gone into the making of so many of those costumes. One pretty blonde in a diaphanous green dress and antlers on her head appeared to be some sort of forest goddess, and even had a pet ferret running up and down her arm and shoulder. I kept worrying that the ferret would make a break for it, but it stayed put. The designers of all these costumes would work on them maybe all year, just to spend a minute parading the results before a panel of three judges and then vanish – at least until the next con. It was impressive.

The next contestant emerged from a room off to one side, and I sat up straight. I'd seen this costume once before.

It was a carrot with legs.

16-

Valerie Clark as Eve: "Maybe people really aren't worth saving."

Gene Barry as Jonathan: "I don't know. A lot of them are nice."- The 27th Day *(1957)*

For the first time, I paid attention to the master of ceremonies – the same one I'd seen last night with the turkey feather in his cap – as he announced the next contestant. "A surprise contestant, who has chosen not to reveal her name just yet, portraying the carrot creature from either *The Thing* or maybe a relative of the cucumber monster from *It Conquered the World*."

The requisite laughs came, followed by polite applause and a couple of shrill male whistles no doubt directed at the legs. The carrot joined the other contestants who had already strutted across the stage and were awaiting the judging results.

I sat back, now committed to stay through the rest of the contest, no matter how long it went. But it didn't go too much longer.

The judges consulted and, after an encore parade of the contestants back and forth across the stage, the M.C. announced their findings. The carrot wasn't among the winners, but that was the one I kept watching to see either whether she would remove the painted shell or where she might go.

She didn't go anywhere for a while. Like a number of the other contestants, she stayed around to pose for pictures, either with other costumers, with one of the fans, or by herself. When all that was over and the contestants began going their separate ways, she went to a corner of the room, bent over and eased the carrot casing off.

She stood up and turned around, and it wasn't Cheyanne at all. It was none other than Dana DuQueen, shaking out her blonde locks and looking quite charming in her tights and abbreviated black top.

"Wow! It's her," various male voices could be heard in the area where Dana had un-costumed herself. She gave them all a big smile, and began chatting with them as they approached diffidently.

I approached, too, having already been started in that direction. I let the young male admirers pretty much finish with their praise and adoration before I barged in. During a lull, I said asked if she had put that costume together herself.

"Oh no," she said, "I saw a lady wearing it last night during the opening ceremonies. I ran into her later and asked if I could borrow it for tonight. I thought it might be fun to slip into the contest without anybody knowing who I was. But naturally I couldn't fool these guys," she said, giving a queenly wave around at the crowd of young males.

"Who did come up with it?" I asked in what I hoped was all innocence.

"She has a most unusual name. Cheyanne Caday, and the spelling is unusual, too. But a very nice lady."

I was afraid my quota of questions was about to be used up, but I put one more to her. "Will she pick up the carrot tonight?"

"I suppose so. She told me just to leave it in here after I'd finished with it. Or she may come by tomorrow and get it." With that, she turned to one of the others in the group to exchange some pleasantries, and I faded away.

I was tempted to sit by that damned carrot all night, but realized that wasn't very practical. Still, I could wander around in its vicinity for a little while. That soon got old, so I found myself a chair near a corner of the room and made a show of checking out some of the apps on my iPhone.

I was still doing it an hour later, and my battery was about to go, when Cheyanne walked in from the hall.

I'd have known her anywhere. Her hair was a little lighter, and she had added some artificial highlights to it. She wore a pair of large-frame glasses which she'd never needed before, but if anything they added to the attractiveness of her wide brown eyes. If she'd put on any weight over the years, I couldn't see it. She wore a dark jacket over a white shirtwaist, and gray slacks that covered those attractive legs but didn't divert attention from them. Not mine, at least. She was walking swiftly in that long, athletic stride I remembered from years ago toward where the carrot shell leaned against a wall.

I got there about the same time she did. "Well, I'd heard that copperheads shed their skins several times a year, but I never knew that carrots did," I said.

She turned around and gave me the same smile I remembered from long ago. "Hey, Simon," she said. "I was hoping I'd run into you again before the weekend was gone."

"I didn't remember the glasses," I said.

"Oh, they're mainly for distance. When I want to see something up close, I take them off," she said, doing so and turning to look at me. We both smiled remembering when we'd both laughed at that line while watching a re-run of the '50s *War of the Worlds* movie, a shared joke that no one besides ourselves would understand or care about.

I couldn't keep my eyes from straying to the third finger of her left hand. No ring.

"Nope, still not married," she said, not missing a thing as usual. "How about you?"

"Nobody would have me," I said.

"Oh, I don't know. You have some special qualities. After all, you're the only guy I ever met who could hum Bernard Herrmann's theremin score to *Day the Earth Stood Still*. No mean accomplishment there."

I smiled, but quickly turned serious. "Annie, are you going to be tied up with work until you're gone, or do you think you could work me in for a little catching up? Maybe tomorrow, if you're not busy all day with your boss."

"I won't be busy with Doctor Allgood at all after this weekend," she said. "I feel as though I've done all I could with his image and bookings and everything. Time to move on, I decided. So I'll be looking for a new gig after things wind up here."

I wondered if Doctor Allgood's performance this weekend, compared to the expectations he'd raised, had anything to do with that decision. But it was none of my business.

"I would really like not to lose touch with you," I blurted out. "I don't want to interfere with whatever you have to do here, but I'd sure like it if you could work me in for a little bit, maybe tomorrow sometime."

"I can work you in right now," she said brightly. "How about some coffee or something? The Regency Room is closed, but the Pine Room will be open for a while."

We parked her carrot in the hallway, in case the lecture hall got locked up for the night, and found ourselves sitting at one of the small pub tables, her with coffee and me with a soft drink. It didn't take me long to catch her up on what I'd been doing since leaving Roanoke, since it was simply one writing assignment after another. She, on the other hand, had moved around among a variety of employers, from a member of Congress to the celebrity scientist with whom she was now finishing up.

"So what's next?" I asked.

"Vacation," she said. "I've been working my tail off for the past two years keeping Doctor Allgood before the public. I've earned a rest."

"Where are you living these days?" I asked.

"Newburgh, New York. It's close to the city, so I can get to the various booking agencies I need to contact…"

"Newburgh! We're practically neighbors. I've been renting a little place in Highland Falls, over near the Military Academy! If only I'd known you were so close by."

"Well, I'm not there, very much. You see where I am right now," she said, laughing. "I don't imagine you're much of a homebody, either."

The time flew by, and the pub would be closing soon. There had been some live entertainment going on, but I was oblivious to it. I knew I wouldn't have the chance to say everything I'd like to, but there was one thing I did want to get off my chest. "I've kicked myself every day since I let you get away," I said before I could think of a better way to say it. Or maybe there was no better way. "All this time, I've been thinking that it was the best thing for you and the position you held, and now…"

"Poor Simon." She laid her hand on top of mine on the little transparent table. "You always did believe the best of people. You never managed to see how messed up so much of the human race could be. Sometimes I wonder how you made it as a journalist, without someone taking advantage."

"The human race has its good points, too," I said. "You taught me that a long time ago."

"Closing time, folks," someone called out from behind the bar. I glanced at my watch and, sure enough, we were into the early morning hours. I got up and went through the motions of easing Cheyanne's chair back for her.

"This was fun," I said. "I hope we can do it again."

"I always told you that you were an optimist," she said, smiling up at me. "But keep the faith. You never know what might happen next."

17—

Cameron Mitchell as Steve: "Doctor Lane, I once heard of a man who climbed a higher mountain than anyone else alive, but he was never able to get down again. What's left of him is still up there."

John Litel as Lane: "The point is, Steve, he made it."
- Flight to Mars, *1951*

I ordered a light breakfast in the Regency Room the next morning, and opened the copy of the newspaper I'd just purchased in the lobby. Nothing on page one, and nothing on the inside of the first section. I skipped the sports and went to the entertainment section.

There it was, and they'd even given me a byline over a "Special to the Roanoke Times" tag. Bagley had managed to add recent wire photos of both Allgood and Chiswell, and sidebars listing their major claims to fame over the years. All in all, it was a pretty good package and, given that the entertainment section was generally done up in advance of the regular deadlines, I wondered how he'd managed it.

Again, my original story had been watered down a bit. I was sure Bagley would have tried to call me to clear the changes – at least that's what he would have done if I was still on the regular staff – but I wasn't in my room to hear the phone, and my cell had drained its battery, until I left it recharging when I went to bed in the wee small hours this morning.

Still, I could see why they handled it the way they had. Delaney had been right. The story did sound crazy, if presented with complete seriousness. So Bagley or someone he supervised rewrote parts of it to make it clear that the opinions expressed in the article were not necessarily those of the paper. But it was still a hell of a what-if? scenario, and I could visualize readers eating it up. I was sure it would make the wire services. Allgood and Chiswell were known in too many other parts of the country beyond the Roanoke Valley.

I could already visualize the knock-off SF writers who would be taking this theme and running with it, setting records for getting novels completed about aliens among us. Not that the concept was anything new for the genre. Everybody from Robert Heinlein and Jack Finney to Chad Oliver and Eric Frank Russell had taken a crack at it, back in the "golden age" days – and even Ray Bradbury, if you counted his uncredited treatment for the screenplay of *It Came from Outer Space*. No doubt many of their books on that topic would be reissued now, but that was a good thing.

My original plan was to stay one more night in Roanoke, after the convention ended, and then fly home. But today was Sunday, and I doubted that Bagley would be working. He could always mail me my check, but I wanted to see the old reprobate in person while I was here. And I definitely wanted to hang around the hotel today, even if Bagley had been in the office, in case Cheyanne turned up again. Postponing my return flight was seeming to me a better idea all the time. I kept looking around the dining room to see if she turned up for breakfast.

The convention would be winding down today. There would probably be more people on the remaining panels than there were in the audiences for each of them. For me, it was pretty well over, anyway. Now that my cover had been blown by the paper, if some of the print-hating managers of the convention recognized my name or figured out who I was, there would probably be a public expulsion. I could just visualize someone in a Starfleet officer's costume breaking my pencil over his knee and tearing my badge in half.

But it was good to have the work all over, especially since the assignment from Bagley had been so vague in the first place. Nobody knew what they were going to get, and Bagley probably wouldn't even have made an effort to try and get it if someone hadn't told him he couldn't. I didn't know myself how much truth there was in what I had written. Delaney's arguments had been more persuasive than I'd been willing to admit. But the paper had handled it all very well, and it was all left for the reader to decide.

I was feeling pretty cocky about accomplishing what I'd set out to do, and it really had been an interesting time. I had enjoyed seeing the changes around the city since I had last been here. I knew I would enjoy laughing about old times with Bagley when we got together. Most of all, I had enjoyed reuniting with Cheyanne, and I kept nursing a hope that it might happen again – if not here, then back in New York where I now knew she lived.

There was something smugly satisfying about getting something done when others had tried to stop you. I knew just how Bagley felt.

It was getting toward 10 in the morning, and the Regency Room would be closing before too much longer as far as breakfast was concerned. I guessed Cheyanne and her party must have dined out elsewhere, again. I signed the check, left a tip, and wandered somewhat aimlessly down the hallway outside the dining room and through a door leading to the outside.

It was a fine, sunny day. I smacked the folded newspaper smartly against my leg, and decided a good walk around the hotel would be just the thing to settle my breakfast. I found myself nodding hello to strangers, and most of them smiled right back, something that was more likely to happen in Roanoke than in New York. God was in his heaven, and all was right with the world.

If I hadn't thrown my head back to take in a breath of fresh air, I would probably never even have seen the silent object that flitted through the blue sky overhead. But I did notice that it seemed to be growing larger, still making no noise at all. It was moving too fast for a balloon, I thought idly. Maybe somebody had marketed a toy drone aircraft for kids to play with.

It didn't have wings, though, I saw as it came down even closer. In fact, if it had any shape at all, I would have called it circular – or disc-shaped, even. A tiny alarm bell was going off somewhere in the back of my mind, but I ignored it. All that was behind me for now. I had better things on my mind.

Then I heard the sound, the nerve-wracking high-pitched screcch, and it seemed to be coming from the object overhead. A few others seemed to be hearing it, too, but they were all looking around from side to side, rather than up. So none of them saw the little blue light that emanated from the bottom of the disc, and seemed to grow ever larger in size as I stared up at it.

Then it enveloped me entirely, and the only sensation I had was one of the most frigid cold I had ever experienced.

18–

Lee Van Cleef as Tom Anderson: "Do you have any idea what you're listening to?"
Peter Graves as Paul Nelson: "London Philharmonic?"
Anderson: "It's Venus."
Nelson: "Uh-huh."
- It Conquered the World, *1956*

"Keep him warm! Keep those blankets around him!"

"Shouldn't we be thinking about a hospital? After all, the last two came out of one in good shape…"

"I know what I'm doing. A hospital wouldn't help this time, not with the jolt he got. We've got to get this medication into him."

"The way he's frozen, you'd break that needle on his

arm."

"Keep rubbing. Even restoring a tiny bit of circulation will help."

"Careful! Watch that hand, you'll break off a finger!"

"Let's face it, he hasn't got a chance. Not with the dose he took out there."

"Shut up! Keep rubbing…"

I thought I recognized at least one of the voices, but my eyes seemed to be frozen shut. The voices faded in and out, occasionally clear but usually muffled. They all sounded as though they were coming through an echo chamber. I remembered hearing a mention of being wrapped in blankets, but I couldn't feel them. I couldn't feel anything.

The memory of that bluish ray came slowly back to me. I remembered the awful sound, as well, but this time it had been farther away and no so harsh. Unpleasant, but not alarming. So much for my well-honed journalistic powers of observation.

"They've gone too far this time. This was obviously meant to be fatal."

"Pretty blatant, too. Daytime, people around. Although no one seems to have actually seen what happened."

"We all know what happened!"

Take it easy, I wanted to tell them. Don't be so upset. What's a little ray-gun zap between friends? If it was okay for Buck Rogers, it should be okay for me. What was the big deal?

Freezing wasn't the worst way to go, I thought. A bit like simply going to sleep, drifting away, leaving the cares of the world behind. The world? Many worlds. *The House of Many Worlds*. Yeah, I'd read a book with that title, back in middle school. I'd read lots of books like that, back in those days.

"Simon, stay with me! Don't let go!"

It would be so easy to drift away. No big deal. Maybe I needed some music to lull me to sleep. Let's see, what would a good title be for a piece of music? *Venus of Dreams* came to me from somewhere. But wait, that wasn't a song, that was another damned book. I bet it would have been a pretty song, though.

"Hang on, Simon!"

Flying saucers. That was a funny way to describe spaceships, or even atmosphere ships from larger spacecraft. Why not flying pots and pans? Now, UFO was a better term. The Air Force was right. After all, what were you going to call a flying saucer that wasn't round? UFO could cover triangular shapes as well, or even square shapes. Or pots and pans. Saucers were the kind of thing that went hay-diddle-diddle, with the cat and the fiddle, and the cow that jumped over the moon, and the dish that ran away with the spoon...

I didn't remember anything for what seemed a long time after that. Although I had no way to measure the time, did I? The blackness could have lasted a micro-second, or it could have gone for eternity. Time didn't matter. Time was an artificial thing we imposed on nature for our own convenience. Time marches on!

Now I was beginning to feel something, and it made me want to go back to my state of blessed numbness. Pins and needles seemed to chase one another throughout my flesh, and they hurt! They hurt a lot!

I began to shake, but there was nothing I could do about it. Shivers on steroids. Was I starting to feel something now? I could sure feel those pins and needles, all over. But something else was touching me, on the outside rather than within. Something rubbed against my arms, my chest, my face. It must have been one of those damned blankets someone had been talking about.

Mill Mountain. Something about Mill Mountain. That's where everything had started. That was where it would end, if it ended at all. But how did I know that? And what was it that would be coming to an end?

It was too much to worry about right now. I was tired, I needed to sleep. Sleep, that knits up the raveled sleeve of care – wasn't that how some line from a play went? And what did "raveled" mean, anyway? Who cared? Sleep…

Something stung my face. Like a slap. Had somebody slapped me? What was the matter with these people? Why couldn't they just leave me alone? Ouch! Damned if somebody didn't do it again!

Now my body was beginning to feel as though someone had burned it with a gigantic branding iron. Was I on fire? Why couldn't they make up their minds, whether to burn me or freeze me? This was beginning to become exasperating. Smack me, will you? Just wait until I can move one of my arms. We'll see who gets slapped.

At least the shakes seemed to have alleviated. And the tingling throughout my skin had become almost bearable now. But I still couldn't move, or even open my eyes.

My right arm was sore. Someone must have jabbed me there, but I didn't remember it. Why was I being treated so nastily? Just wait until I get up off this bed, I'll lick you all…

Bed? I guess I must have been on a bed. A flat surface, anyway, and not uncomfortable. In fact, I could feel myself roll a bit to one side, then the other. It felt pretty good. I tried a few other moves. Flexed my fingers. Wiggled my toes. Wrinkled my nose. Opened my eyes…

Cheyanne's lovely face completely filled my field of vision. She bent even closer, and I could feel, yes, *feel*, her soft lips on mine. Warmth was spreading through me now, a wonderful warmth, the kind you get from an open fire, or lying on a sunny beach, or from the lips of the woman you love.

19—

James Arness as FBI Agent Bob Graham: "And I thought today was the end of them."

Edmund Gwenn as Doctor Harold Medford: "No. We haven't seen the end of them. We've only had a close view of the beginning of what may be the end of us."
- THEM!, *1953*

The hotel room where I woke up was very much like mine, but I knew it wasn't the same one. For one thing, it had two beds instead of one. I lay on one of them, covered to my chin. Sun streamed in through one window. Now I understood the old cliché that had people waking up and wondering first thing: Where am I?

I seemed to be alone in the room. "Hello?" I said. Or tried to say. My voice came out cracked and faint. "Hello?" A little better that time, but still no response.

There was a sudden urge for me to get to the bathroom. Had I downed too much of a soft drink last night? I threw back the covers with some little effort, and found myself naked. Well, that would make it easier for what I had to do in the toilet.

But a wave of dizziness swept over me when I tried to sit up and swing my legs over the edge of the bed. I sat still until it passed, which it did, finally. I pushed myself to my feet, my hands on either side giving me impetus from the mattress. Very carefully, I made my way to the facility, took care of business, and flushed.

Now what? I found a glass by the lavatory, filled it with water, rinsed my mouth and then swallowed some. It tasted pretty good. I put the glass down carefully, and made my way back to the bed. I sat for a few minutes, then got up again and began rummaging through drawers and hangars. I found a variety of clothes, but none of them were mine. Not unless I'd had a sex-change operation while I was out.

I peeled off one of the thinner blankets from the bed, and wrapped myself in it. I wasn't cold, just modest. Apparently this room belonged to a woman.

I didn't want to look a gift horse in the mouth, but how exactly had I ended up here? I tried to think back – writing the newspaper story, finding Cheyanne, going to the pub, going back to my room, getting up the next day, showering, shaving, breakfast, going for a walk outdoors…

The flying saucer! The blue ray!

That was as far back as I could go. Had it been real? Or had I been so wrapped up in this business that now I was having nightmares about it?

The door opened. I pulled the blanket tighter, and then Cheyanne came through it. "Oh!" she said, startled. "Simon, I didn't think you would wake up for at least two more hours. I would never have left the room."

She was carrying a cardboard cup of coffee, which she placed on the dresser before she came to me. She put her arms around me, and it was all I could do to keep from dropping the blanket to hug her back.

She sat me down on a corner of the bed, then retrieved the coffee. "Here," she said. "You need this more than I do."

It did taste good, and its warmth seemed to flow down to the core of my body. "You're right, I did need that," I said. "Thanks." My voice still wasn't strong, but at least it had become recognizable as mine.

She sat down on the bed beside me. "How much do you remember?" she asked.

"I think I was zapped outside by a flying saucer."

"That's right. Good. Then I guess you remember everything."

"I don't remember how I wound up in your room. This is your room, isn't it?"

"Our room, for now. The convention ended three days ago, and your reservation expired after that. I found your airline reservation in your dresser, and cancelled your flight. You can re-book when you're ready."

"Wait a minute." I took a deep breath. "I really was zapped by a flying saucer?"

"Indeed, you were. And they weren't fooling around. They didn't want you just incapacitated, they wanted you removed permanently."

"I thought that was all over," I said.

"No. It may just be starting."

"I guess it would be an understatement to say I don't

understand."

"Of course you don't. How could you? Even we didn't see it coming."

"We? Who's we?"

Cheyanne took a deep breath, and turned those expressive brown eyes directly on me. "We, the survivors from that first landing."

Even though I was sitting, the world seemed to rock beneath me. I understood her words, but it took me some time to absorb their meaning.

"You're…from…"

"Yes, out there, far out there. I'll tell you all about it one day. Right now, we have more pressing concerns."

"Doctor Allgood," I began. "Is he one of you?"

She smiled. "No, he's one of you. But there was a reason why I was working for him, the same reason why I worked for a man on a congressional technology committee before him, and a number of others before that. I was doing what I could to bring your people up to speed so others couldn't set you back."

"But Allgood knew, didn't he?"

"Only for the past month. That was why he planned to take the first step in making your people aware of our presence, by talking about it here and letting the belief and understanding filter out slowly enough so your people could eventually accept it."

"So that was why he spoke to me so freely out there on the King Memorial Bridge," I said, almost to myself. "When I told him you'd vouch for me, he took that to mean I was in on your secret, too."

"Yes. He probably thought you had taken my place, because I'd let him down. I had assured him he would be safe in making his announcement. And when you saved him, he must have believed that you were another of our people."

"How many of you are here?"

"Only three, now. Only myself, in the United States. I had no idea that the others would take such drastic action to try and stop our gradual revelation about our having lived among you. I guess the others must have some very different design."

"Are you and the others in touch with each other?"

"Not at all. I don't even know who any of them are, or how many they are. Or, most of all, why they've gone to such drastic measures to keep it all from coming out. With the devices they've been using, they have all but given the truth away themselves."

"And it's not over," I said.

"No. We may be entering a totally new phase now, and, for the first time, I have no idea how it will all come out."

20—

Walter Brooke as General Merritt: "It's my personal conviction that no one but an idiot would volunteer, and I shall strongly suspect the sanity of anyone who does. All right, we've all got it straight. Who wants to go?"
- Conquest of Space, *1955*

Doctor Allgood, Cheyanne told me, had departed when the convention had ended. She was confident that he wouldn't reveal her identity, but he would continue to promote the idea that We Are Not Alone. That fit right into his own ideas, and he would probably have been promoting much the same things, anyway. Cheyanne had simply helped guide him to this point, and then revealed the truth about herself to him.

I was dressed, now. Cheyanne had rescued my belongings from my former room, packed them up and brought them here. If I'd recognized my own suitcase, I could have put something on immediately.

"What about Professor Chiswell?" I asked.

"Strangely enough, he's still here," she said. "I can't imagine why. Like Doctor Allgood, he should be making the talk show rounds promoting his own ideas."

"But you never revealed yourself to Chiswell?"

"No. I had to choose which of your public icons would best serve our purposes, and I decided it was Doctor Allgood. Professor Chiswell is too wedded to his own self-promotion to accept any direction from us."

"I'm not so sure."

Cheyanne turned her intent look on me. "What do you mean?"

"I think he's been contacted by the others. Or whoever the other visitors are."

She nodded. "Possibly. Dr. Allgood was convinced that the apparent attack on Chiswell was staged, just for credibility when the same thing was supposed to happen the next day to Dr. Allgood."

"I'm betting Allgood would have gotten the full force of that freeze stuff, just the way I did. It wouldn't have been a dose from which he could recover, like Chiswell, and like…"

Cheyanne watched me for a few seconds. "Like…"

"Annie, why would these others zap a kid? If they've been around for half a century and nobody's caught on, what could some kid at a science fiction convention happen upon that would threaten them?"

"I don't know. But they did, in fact, zap him, as you put it."

"And they zapped Chiswell. Maybe for the same reason

you mentioned: credibility."

"I…don't understand, Simon."

"And why did they try for me? I'd already done everything I was going to do in this little venture. Unless they thought I was onto something else."

"Why would they think that?"

"I have a just a vague idea. But I think I know who can help me make it clear. If I can talk him into it."

It took me a while to reach Investigator Delaney. He was apparently a very busy man. But I finally did get him, and asked if I could come to the city police department for a talk.

"I'm not sure I want my bosses to see me with you," Delaney said. "I don't want them to think that I'm a nutcase, too."

"Well, how about if you come to the hotel? I'll even buy you dinner."

"I've had enough of that place, too. Tell you what. I've got some overtime, I can get off duty around four this afternoon. How about if I meet you at a Dunkin' Donuts place? You know all cops love donuts."

"That sounds okay."

"There's one on Keagy Road and one on Franklin. Either one suits me."

I thought it over. "The one on Franklin Road – that's not far from Mill Mountain, is it?"

"Not too far, no," Delaney said.

"Let's meet there. We just might want to make a side trip to Mill Mountain afterward."

"Mill Mountain? What's that all about?"

"I'll tell you when I see you. Oh, and one other thing – I wonder if you could check on a certain patient who was lately at Community Hospital?"

21—

Richard Denning as Rick: "All I know is there are two forms of life fighting for survival here in this valley, and only one of them can win." - Day the World Ended, 1955

I had planned to call a cab again, but Cheyanne insisted I was not going to leave her behind. So we ended up in a little black Smart Car that she'd rented, with its nine-gallon gas tank and three-cylinder motor. "Annie, I know there are flying saucers in your past, but I hadn't planned to take a ride with you in one," I said.

"Relax, you'll like it. The two seats are full size. It's just the rest of the car that's squashed."

She drove us all the way to Franklin Road, and we pulled off to the left into the Dunkin' Donuts parking lot. Delaney was already there, seated at one of the outdoor tables with a little pink umbrella sticking up from its middle, enjoying a chocolate-covered donut.

I introduced Cheyanne, and added: "Would you mind if we go inside? I've gotten a little nervous about the great outdoors lately."

He shrugged, wiped his fingers with a napkin, and followed us in. Cheyanne and I each ordered ice coffee, and Delaney got a couple more donuts. I guess what he said about cops and donuts was true, at least in his case.

He took a bite from one of the donuts, chewed thoughtfully, and said, "Okay. I'm here. What's all this sensitive information that you want to impart to me?"

"First, let me ask you one. Did you have a chance to do that checkup at the hospital?"

"Yeah." He took another bite. "And you were right, it was pretty strange. Jimmy Cox was in the place for almost twenty-four hours, and none of the staff saw hide nor hair of his parents. They never could reach them. Jimmy said they didn't have a land-line phone, but he could call them on his cell."

"So did he?"

"If he did, they never made it to the hospital."

"Kind of strange, wouldn't you say?"

"You meet all kinds in this business," he said. "Although I sure wouldn't nominate them for Parents of the Year."

"Can you be sure they even exist?"

"Well, the attending physician took the responsibility for signing him in and releasing him. I imagine he was in contact with the family."

"Is that the same doctor that you yourself said turned up so conveniently when Jimmy and Professor Chiswell had to be treated?"

"Oh, so now you're going to throw my wandering

thoughts back at me, huh?" He took another bite. "Just what are you getting at, anyway?"

I leaned forward. "You read the article I turned in before it got watered down for public distribution. Can you, just for the sake of argument, pretend that it might all have been true?"

Delaney polished off the first donut and picked up the second. "I don't know. That's a mighty big stretch."

"It fits the explanation you tried to give me. Only it proves something you probably didn't expect."

"Well, I came down here, so there's no point in not hearing you out. Go ahead."

"Suppose there was more than one faction of aliens living as residents of the Roanoke Valley? One side contacted Allgood, working with him to spin out his aliens-among-us thing, the one he was going to talk about at the convention. That side wants us thinking along those lines so we can acclimate ourselves to the idea."

"Go on."

"The other faction wants the secrecy to continue. They'd rather have less serious people out there pushing the aliens theory, if anybody has to push it. They know Chiswell would never be taken seriously, so they got him invited to give his spiel, figuring the two would probably cancel one another out as far as public acceptance was concerned."

"Uh-huh. Don't stop now." He took another bite. I glanced at Cheyanne. She was hanging on every word, too.

"Maybe Chiswell was getting out of control, I don't know. Anyway, they wanted to give him a warning. And whatever they did to him would pave the way for doing something similar to Allgood, when he was getting ready to give his version of things."

Cheyanne spoke up. "Simon, I see what you're saying. They decided any kind of revelation like that, believed or not, would be too dangerous. They wanted to pull the plug on both talks."

"And they managed to get the technology in place to do it, too. I don't pretend to know how any of it works. Indistinguishable from magic, you know."

"But they wanted to make sure it worked the way they wanted, that they could regulate it," she said. "So they tried it out on the Cox boy first."

"Maybe," I said. "But then, why did they make a run at me?"

"Run at you? What's that about?" Delaney asked.

I told him what happened. "If Allgood and Cheyanne hadn't figured out how to help me recover, I wouldn't be here now."

Delaney closed his eyes, and used a napkin to wipe the last of the donut crumbs from his lips. He opened them again. "A flying saucer, huh? And nobody else saw it, I'll bet."

"Nobody else reported it, anyway," I said. "If you saw one, would you report it?"

"What, and get kicked off…?" He stopped, and pursed his lips. "Okay, good point. No, I probably wouldn't. Who would I report it to, anyway? The Bureau of Missing Dishes?"

"But again, Simon," Cheyanne said. "Why would they be after you?"

"Because I made a bad mistake. In all innocence, I braced the alien in his human persona. I did it in all innocence. I thought maybe he'd have some information I could use to corroborate the other things I'd been working on. But then he made an even worse mistake. He jumped to the conclusion that I knew more than I did, that I had identified him. And, to him, that was a capital offense."

"I'm pretty sure I know what you're going to say," Delaney said. "But go ahead. Just who is this alien in disguise?"

Cheyanne said it before I did. "Jimmy Cox. The boy who seemed to have been the first person to be attacked."

"What better cover could he have?" I said. "Something very strange, but apparently non-lethal, was going on around the hotel. But then it turned lethal, assuming Allgood was meant not to recover. But then it went away. You hear about weird stuff like that a lot. There would be nothing for any health officials to find afterward. It would just be one of those unsolved mysteries."

"All right," Delaney said. "It all sounds like a crock to me. But suppose, just suppose, everything you say is true. What can you do about it? Wait for him to come along and do a better job on you next time?"

"Exactly," I said.

"What?" Cheyanne looked at me. "Simon, no."

"Well, I don't mean I want him to do a better job," I said. "But I do want him to make another try. And I know just the place for him to do it."

22—

Michael Granger as Frank Buchanan: "Is he dead?"
Gregory Gaye as Dr. Steigg: "He never was alive."
- Creature with the Atom Brain, *1955*

I could hear the electrical hum running through the giant neon tubing that composed the artificial star atop Mill Mountain. Light from the star cast almost enough light for me to see my shadow.

But not enough to see the man shadowing me.

I knew he was there, though. As I'd told Cheyanne and Delaney, he'd been there for the past week.

He wasn't very good at it. He might be the product of some extraterrestrial intelligence, but he didn't know much about following someone without being seen. Of course, I did have the advantage of knowing that he'd be there.

I hadn't had to find him. He had found me, even before Cheyanne and I got into her car. He had stayed behind us all the way from the hotel to the Dunkin' Donuts shop. And when she drove me up the mountain to Riverland Road, and into the parking lot past the Mill Mountain Star Trail sign to drop me off, he'd been right on our tail.

No remote control this time, I thought. No ceiling to hide a weapon for a shot at someone on a stage. No flying disc to try and pinpoint me from the air. He probably wondered why that hadn't worked, because he had to know I'd been struck full-on by the beam from above. He had not counted on Cheyanne forcing together a team of people to pull me through.

I wonder if he knew who Cheyanne really was. I hoped not, and I didn't think so. After all, Cheyanne hadn't realized who he was.

The shell which was Jimmy Cox still looked to me, for all the world, like someone who had tried out and failed for a job with the Bowery Boys. I didn't know what kind of support system he had in place. He had obviously managed to create records of sort for himself – school, Social Security, all of that, no real trick for the kind of technology which had spawned him, I imagined.

It had been easy to follow the uphill signs, to where the trail went into the woods and across Fishburn Parkway. Now I could see the viewing platform next to the gigantic star.

All I had to do was wait.

I didn't have to wait long. I could hear his footsteps coming up the trail behind me. Where was Delaney? I hadn't seen him, not at all. I hoped he'd managed to keep up with us, because I was counting on him to keep me from being frozen for good this time. Frozen, or something else that the creature within Jimmy might have come up with.

Maybe I was being foolish to count on Delaney. He had seemed to go along with what I was saying, but what if he was just humoring me? Humor the crazy man who believes he's being stalked by aliens. Sure, Simon, I'll follow and make sure the big bad E.T. doesn't do something bad to you, don't worry. And then, as I drive away with Cheyanne, he shakes his head sadly and thinks, Good riddance.

Is that what had really happened?

I wondered what it was about the mountain that drew the visitors from the first landing to it, and then all the ones that followed. Did magnetic lines of force detectable only by some higher technologies cross here? Was this some sort of extraterrestrial holy place? Was it the artificial star itself, erected only a year before the first arrival, which exerted some kind of an attraction? From a human perspective, the five-pointed star was a symbol of a sun and all the other suns that twinkled light years away in the sky overhead, but how could aliens know that?

There had been a few other people on the Mill Mountain Star Trail this evening, but they were long gone by now. There was a nip in the air tonight, nothing anyone would want to stay out in for too long. I might have stayed out in it too long myself.

Where was Delaney?

The bravado that I'd managed to convey back at the Dunkin' Donuts shop, about setting myself up as bait right where the others would feel most at home, had long since leached away. It felt as though I was up here by myself, now – by myself as far as human company was concerned.

I had long since stopped thinking of Jimmy Cox as human.

Cheyanne hadn't wanted me to try this trap. She didn't trust Delaney to be on the spot in time, either. We had given him plenty of time to get up here ahead of us, before we left the Dunkin' Donuts place ourselves. But if he was here, I certainly didn't see him.

Well, I shouldn't be able to see him, I told myself. If I could have seen him, the Jimmy creature would probably have spotted him, too. And then this would have all been for nothing.

A figure came shuffling out of the woods. Its stringy blond hair was askew, and it had no expression on his face whatsoever. Its arms hung at its sides, no weapon in sight. It came toward me, dragging its feet like an automaton. The face looked like Jimmy's, but there was no animation in it. Nothing in the eyes, the mouth a mere slit, and then it struck me.

This wasn't the Jimmy creature at all. This was a construct of some kind made to look like Jimmy.

Was it a robot of some sort, a decoy? Was the real Jimmy up here watching me from somewhere else, waiting to make sure there was no trap set for him? Had he known all along what I was trying to do, and had just been playing me? Maybe this construct that was coming toward me was some sort of walking bomb, ready to detonate as soon as it got close enough to make sure the explosion would take me with it.

Whatever it was, I didn't want any part of it. I began circling away from it, trying to get back toward the woods, where maybe, just maybe, the trees might shield me from whatever device that thing was using to track me.

As soon as I started moving, it stopped dead in its tracks. One hand raised toward me, finger extended, like a grade school kid playing a game of cowboys, where they "shot" at each other with their fingers, mouthing "chee" "chee" sounds to substitute for gunshots.

And then I could hear something warming up, something which drowned out the hum of the neon tubing overhead, something that was coming from within the Jimmy construct, as its finger zeroed in on where I stood. For an instant, I could see a white light at the end of that finger, pointing right at me.

And then a beam stabbed out from it, not unlike the beam of incandescence manifested from the robot Gort in *The Day the Earth Stood Still*. But this was no special-effects beam, added to a movie film after the actors all hit their spots for the live action part. This was the real stuff, baby, not a freeze-ray or anything like that, but something new that the others had come up with, something which would probably reduce me to ash and leave nothing but a few fragments for the winds up on the mountain to blow away.

The light was blinding, and there was nothing I could do to stop it.

23—

Kenneth Tobey as Captain Mathews: "We explode our torpedo and get blown apart ourselves – or we think faster than we've ever thought before."
- It Came from Beneath the Sea, *1955*

I did the only thing I could think to do. I hit the ground, as flat as I could.

I could feel the heat of the beam sizzle over where I lay, and then it stopped. I looked up, and saw that the Jimmy construct was re-aiming its finger to where I lay prone. I tried rolling to one side, but his finger merely tracked my movement, and I could hear the internal humming from within the figure again as it warmed up for a second and final shot at me.

Then there was a bang, and the figure became a focus of light that ranged outward and then inward again, like a silent explosion that left me with spots before my eyes. I blinked, unable to see clearly for a moment. When my vision finally started acclimating to the darkness again, there was nothing standing in front of me. The Jimmy-thing was gone, completely gone.

"Gee-zuss!" I heard the exclamation behind me. "What the hell was that thing?"

Delaney came crawling out from behind one of the small trees growing beneath the star, a nasty-looking automatic in his right hand. The spots were still there but fading fast, as I blinked dumbly at the investigator.

"I thought you'd decided not to be here," I said hoarsely.

He ignored me, walking past to where the blinding light had flowed and ebbed, leaving no trace of its source. He examined the ground where the Jimmy construct had stood. It hadn't even left ashes behind to blow away.

"I was aiming at the center of his mass," Delaney said. "I don't know what I hit, but it certainly did the job."

"If he'd gotten closer, he, it, could've taken me along," I said, my voice starting to sound almost normal again. "Maybe that was the original idea, and the finger thing was just a backup."

"I don't know," Delaney said, shaking his head. "Seems to me either one would've done the job."

We stood there for maybe five minutes, both of us trying to come to terms with what we'd just seen. Finally, Delaney stirred. He looked down at the pistol in his hand as though he'd forgotten it was there. He stuck it back into his hip-holster, and let the flap of his coat drop over it.

"Come on," he said. "Let's get the hell out of here."

The walk back down the mountain seemed to take even longer than when I'd come up. I found myself peering on either side of the trail to make sure there was no movement in the woods alongside. Did that automaton guide itself in some way? Or was Jimmy still here somewhere, from some point where he had operated it himself?

But nobody jumped out at us, nothing happened, and I was soon seated in Delaney's car and headed back to the city.

"What kind of police report are you going to write about this?" I asked, trying to contain a giggle which I was afraid might grow out of control.

"Report? Are you kidding? 'Tracked one E.T. to the top of Mill Mountain. Destroyed same when it tried to burn someone down with its finger. No trace of anything at all to substantiate any part of what I'm saying.' Oh sure, I can just see me making out a report on this."

Delaney came with me up to the room where I'd awakened earlier that day. That day? I couldn't believe it had all been less than a day. It seemed like I had lived a year in the past few hours.

Cheyanne let us in, and grabbed me in a ferocious hug. "Thank goodness," she whispered. "You're back."

"And in one piece," Delaney said, pausing in the hallway outside the door. "But I can't say as much for Jimmy."

I looked at him. "Did you think that was Jimmy?" I asked.

"Well, Jimmy, or whatever creature was existing inside of him. Let's not get technical about it."

"But that wasn't Jimmy, or his creature. That was a mechanism of some kind, made to look like Jimmy."

"A what?"

"Oh, no," breathed Cheyanne. "Then we didn't get him,

after all."

"Now wait a minute," Delaney protested. "I saw him. It must have been Jimmy…"

"You didn't see it as closely as I did," I told him. "It was some kind of look-alike, a walking weapon. It wasn't meant to come back. It was meant to disappear the way it did, only it was supposed to take me with it."

"Then…what? We have the thing to do all over again?" said Delaney.

"I don't know," I said. "I don't know what we can do. I'll have to think about it."

24—

John Archer as Barnes: "Now look, there's no law against taking off a spaceship: it's never been done, so they haven't got around to prohibiting it."
- Destination: Moon, *1950*

"At least all this has made a believer out of Delaney," I said. "He'll be back here this morning so we can figure out our next step."

"I think our next step should involve Professor Chiswell," Cheyanne said.

Last night had been just a bit awkward for both of us. It wasn't as though Cheyanne and I had never shared a room, but that had been years ago. Of course, I'd been sharing this room with her for the past few days, but I'd been unconscious all that time. Now, I was all too conscious of her proximity, and found myself wondering if I should suggest stepping outside while she dressed for bed.

As usual, she seemed to read my mind.

"Are you going to look at me differently now, Simon?" she asked. "Now that you know that what you see wasn't anything like I looked originally?"

"You should know, by now, that I have no problem whatever with your appearance," I said.

"Well, if you're going to start trying to find where the seams and zippers are located and where the antennae retract, you're going to be out of luck," she said, a smile barely touching her lips. "What you see is actually how I am, lungs, heart, brain, skin and all. We had bio-engineering techniques that our kind developed long ago. We recreated and literally grew Earth bodies into which we could transplant our own consciousness." She looked at me, and turned around as though modeling the blouse and skirt she was wearing. "I'm like this from now on. And, believe it or not, by this time, I'm as used to it as you are used to your body."

It was a lot for me to take in. But I thought I could manage.

"What about Jimmy's kind?" I finally thought to ask. "Was he, ah, *born* the same way?"

"We've never been certain," she said. "We don't know where in the galaxy they come from, just as we've kept the location of our own home planet from them. We don't really know their natural state, and I can't imagine that they know ours. But those of us who volunteered for this mission to Earth knew it was a permanent assignment. Some of us have already died, and been interred like any other human." She walked over and put her arms around me. "I just wanted you to know that what you'd be getting was forever – if you still want it."

I don't think I want to tell you anything about the rest of the night.

Delaney agreed with Cheyanne's idea when he joined us the next morning, over a room service breakfast. The fact that Professor Chiswell was still here meant he was playing some kind of role in whatever the Jimmy creature was doing.

"You'll be glad to know I finally did run down the doctor who looked at Jimmy and Chiswell," Delaney said. "I suppose he could have constructed a false identity like Jimmy, but I've checked back on where he was born, went to school, when he got married, when he got his medical degree, and I'm as certain as it's possible to be in something like this that he has been on this planet all his life." He shook his head. "Damn, it seems weird to talk about this stuff."

"Then his treatment of Jimmy and the professor was just straightforward, medically?" asked Cheyanne.

"I pulled his hospital reports on them," Delaney said. "He seems as baffled as we were over what happened to them, but he treated the symptoms and felt that that did the trick. I don't think we have to worry about him as an enemy creature, or anything like that."

"If that thing last night was operating on its own," I said, "it may be that Jimmy doesn't know I'm still alive and kicking. We might be able to use that."

"Yes, he probably believes he is in the clear, now," Cheyanne agreed. "So we don't want Professor Chiswell to see you, either. Not until we know the relationship between the two of them."

"On the other hand," I said, "maybe his seeing me will help us determine what that relationship is."

The plan we concocted was elegant in its simplicity. Delaney went to Chiswell's room, knocked on his door, flashed his badge, and brought him back to us.

Sure enough, he blanched when I walked in from the bathroom. Delaney had sat the professor down in a chair in the middle of the room, and we could all see his reaction when he first spotted me.

"But he said…"

"He said I was dead, didn't he?" I said matter-of-factly. "You've thrown your lot into the wrong camp, Professor. We humans are onto you, now. It's only a matter of time before we round up Jimmy and any others like him."

I could almost see Chiswell recalculating his situation, behind those heavy-lidded eyes.

"There aren't any others," he said, finally. "Jimmy – I still think of him as Jimmy, although I know he's something else – is the last of them. The others have all died, in one way or another. This world is a scary place for them."

Delaney proved skilled at drawing out details from someone he was interrogating. We heard how Jimmy had approached Chiswell a year ago. It had taken some time for Jimmy to convince Chiswell of his origin. He actually had to shift back into his original form before the professor believed him.

"So, he's a shape-shifter," Delaney mused. "I wonder what sort of crazy evolutionary process resulted in that?"

Jimmy's only goal now was to prevent the knowledge of his presence on this world, Chiswell said. Jimmy had figured out what Doctor Allgood's revelation was going to be. Everything Allgood been doing and saying on the talk show circuit was obviously leading up to it. Jimmy figured that someone from one of the other camps of visitors had been helping Allgood, because some of astronomical tidbits he'd been dropping during his appearances were things he couldn't have known on his own.

"All Jimmy wants to do now is return to his home world, with the certainty that no one is left here knowing about him. I told you about him losing all his counterparts. They were careless, they didn't last long in their Earthly personas. He wants to tell his people to stay away from Earth. His worst fear is that, if we develop a star drive, we will eventually reach his world and do to it what we're doing to this one."

"How does he plan to return?" I asked.

"He has a ship…"

Somehow, it was no surprise to find that the ship was concealed beneath the surface of Mill Mountain. Now that Jimmy believed he had eliminated me, he felt he could leave safely, with nobody left knowing that his world was out there.

"He'd be leaving you behind, Professor," Cheyanne reminded him.

"He knows he can trust me," Chiswell said. "He knows I'd never betray him."

"But you just did," Delaney reminded him.

Chiswell's mouth opened, but nothing came out.

"So," I said, "the question becomes, how do we send Jimmy on his way free of all agitation?"

25—

The flying saucer departed at dawn.

"We could just kill him," Delaney had said, back when we had Chiswell a temporary prisoner in Cheyanne's and my room and were trying to decide about Jimmy.

All three of us protested at that. "Besides, there's a practical reason," Cheyanne said. "If he goes back and reports that Earth is too dangerous to meddle with, they will leave this world alone. If he doesn't go back, there's always a chance his people will send another expedition."

"And we really don't want a bunch of shape-changers coming here with chips on their shoulders," I added.

"You don't really think that he would…eliminate me, before he goes, to protect his secret?" Chiswell asked Delaney.

It was Cheyanne who answered. "I think that would raise more problems for him than it would solve, Professor. You're too prominent. If you died mysteriously, or even disappeared, there would be investigations into what you'd been doing lately. Jimmy's role in that might come out. He has been feeding you some of these revelations that have subsequently been confirmed, hasn't he?"

Chiswell nodded. "Just as one of the other groups has been doing for Allgood," he said defensively.

None of us said it, but I believe we were all thinking that, with Chiswell's reputation for hyperbole, the Jimmy creature would never worry about him being believed even if he did claim contact with an alien.

It was Cheyanne who finally came up with our solution.

All it would take was me making up a news story and getting it in the paper, and Delaney falsifying a police report.

It took some doing, but I finally convinced Bagley that I'd just happened to be in the right place at the right time to get the story. I'd been hiking on Mill Mountain when it happened.

Apparently a youngster named Jimmy Cox, a street person of sorts, apparently something of a loner because not many people knew of him, managed to put together a home-made bomb apparently intending to blow up the Mill Mountain Star.

A witness had seen a boy meeting his description going up the mountain shortly before the explosion. He identified an artist's sketch of what Jimmy looked like. Several people remembered him attending a science fiction convention the previous week, but no one knew much about him.

"I think he bought one of my photos and had me autograph it," said Dana DuQueen, an actress who had been a guest at the convention. "The poor boy. I had no idea he might be mentally unbalanced."

I quoted from the police report by Inspector Delaney that the bomb must have gone off prematurely, and taken the boy with it. There hadn't been enough left of him to bury. But the Mill Mountain Star, thankfully, escaped damage.

And the Jimmy creature, convinced that all traces of his alter ego had been put to rest, left our world behind him the next morning.

There was some puzzlement about the gaping hole that hikers found a few days later on the mountain. The terrain didn't look like it had any sinkholes, but nobody could think of any other explanation.

Only a few people claimed to have seen a flying saucer that morning. Nobody paid them much attention.

"Folks, it's been interesting," Delaney told us, when he gave us a lift to the airport a day later. "But I hope I never have anything to do with another convention like this one."

"We may be back, if they have it next year," I told him. "We'll look you up."

He looked at us, and smirked, probably at the way we were holding hands. "By then, there may be another one of you," he said.

"I hadn't thought of that," I said to Cheyanne. "I mean, can we…?"

"According to Edgar Rice Burroughs, it didn't pose any problems for John Carter and Dejah Thoris," she said.

Delaney shook his head in disgust. "That's all I need," he said. "More of that sci-fi stuff!"

ABOUT THE AUTHOR

Paul Dellinger is a retired newspaper reporter from The Roanoke Times. He has written fiction, radio plays, a stage play performed at Barter Theatre, the State Theater of Virginia, and a non-fiction book (with co-author Danny Gordon), *Don't Look Up!* on the effects of a UFO flap on a small town. His previous book, *Mr. Lazarus and Other Stories*, collects 24 of his previously-published works. He also co-authored, with Tom Angleberger, the middle-school science fiction book, *Fuzzy*. He and his wife, Maxine, live in Wytheville, Viriginia. They have two grown children, Mark and Katie; their spouses, Cindy and David, and grandchildren, Grace and Emma.

www.ingramcontent.com/pod-product-compliance
Lightning Source LLC
Chambersburg PA
CBHW070937130626
46555CB00001B/468